Summer of Love Flashbacks

Louis-Bertrand Labenhe

Library of Congress Cataloging–in–Publication Data
Author: Louis-Bertrand Labeuhe
Title: Summer of Love Flashbacks
Includes an index and a chronology
1. Summer of Love 2. Haight-Ashbury 3. Hippies 4. Counterculture

ISBN-13: 978-2-919405-07-7

First edition

Published by Le Diable Ermite
16 La Petite Rue
55140 Brixey-aux-Chanoines, France
https://le-diable-ermite.blog4ever.xyz

10 9 8 7 6 5 4 3 2 1

To Dominique and the people of Ukraine, *Lux æterna*

Table of Contents

Publisher's Note

The text for *Summer of Love Flashbacks* was created from the personal notebooks and papers of Louis-Bertrand Labeuhe found at his former address on Waller Street, in San Francisco, California. Considerable editing was necessary to make a readable copy of these notes. Moreover, since the documents were handwritten, many parts had to be interpreted. Labeuhe's documents were not always dated, but the events described helped to establish a reasonably close timeframe. It is important to point out that the authenticity of specific events and episodes cannot be confirmed, but many of the persons described in his notebooks did in fact exist, though the existence of some is impossible to verify today.

1

The First Joint

My first experience with marijuana was in high school. That was back in the sixties, in 1964 to be precise. Before that first joint, alcohol was my only means of getting high, or stoned, as we liked to say. Of course, the effect of tetrahydracannabinal (THC) on the human body is not at all like alcohol, which is a depressant. Grass is a euphoriant, in other words it creates feelings of extreme happiness and well-being, something that alcohol never did for me or my friends. On the contrary, excessive consumption of that drug often resulted in feelings of aggressivity and irascibility, although it is widely used to escape banality and the tedious present. More on that later. . . .

Things were really starting to change that year, and more and more young people were discovering dope. It goes without saying that music was a big part of the sixties cultural revolution, which, in many ways, began with the Beatles in 1962 and 1963 with songs like

"Love Me Do," "She Loves You" or "I Want to Hold Your Hand," and then there was the film *A Hard Day's Night* in 1964. Dozens of their songs were hits around the world, but there's no point in trying to mention them all here. Their hair was a big deal because young guys saw that they could let their hair grow long, too. And it had a strong emotional effect on the girls who screamed like crazy lunatics when John, Paul, George and Ringo shook their mop-tops, a direct reference to the household instrument used to wash floors. I never went to a Beatles' concert myself in the USA because there was so much screaming goin' on you couldn't hear the music. It was *really* annoying, you know, a royal pain in the ass. The Fab Four was pissed off, too, because the girls in the audience were not interested in listening to the music.

As far as the hair is concerned, before the Beatles entered the music scene, young people often had short hair called a crew cut, like in the army, or they put grease, wax or special creams in their hair like Brylcream, whose television commercials showed passionate women being seduced by men who used it, and the advert warned men not to use too many dabs of the stuff, because it made women sexually uncontrollable when they put their fingers in men's hair. It was stupid, but there were a lot of inane commercials on TV at the time as consumer culture exploded, and sexual fantasies were a big part of it all. So because of Beatlemania, guys started changing their hairstyles, letting their hair grow longer. For teenagers in high school, this could have consequences because school authorities, habitually narrow-minded and ultra-conservative, enforced arbitrary dress and personal appearance codes. Guys were prevented from going to school if their hair came below their ears, and girls could not wear pants, but had to wear skirts or dresses that had to be a certain length. There was always the Vice Principal or some other jerk waiting at the entrance to make sure the codes were obeyed. I was sent home a couple of times because my hair was too long, and girls with short skirts were sent home, too. These expulsions were always followed by official letters signed by the school authorities informing parents of the blatant misconduct on our part, and the necessity to acknowledge our transgression of the rules by signing the letter before we could return to school. The old geezers who were posted like sentinels to watch students in the morning as they arrived were habitually arrogant and pugnacious, clearly eager to execute their frivolous authority. This domineering attitude was not an exception, but a general rule in high schools and universities. Students accepted the administration's shitty way of doing things because they didn't have any choice. "It's the highway or my way," they'd say, but a few students sought revenge in various ways that need not be explained here. But I can assure you that high school adolescents can be *very* resourceful when it comes to reprisals.

The Vice President in charge of discipline, one Joseph Rance, took sadistic pleasure in harassing students, and no one in the administration was more despised than him by students. Rance had an exceptionally thin face and wore his hair in a greasy pompadour. With his mouth habitually twisted into a frown, his fish eyes, Dumbo ears that stuck out to the side of his head like wings, and long weasel-like head, he was the epitome of contempt. His favorite pastime was haranguing students with short, choppy phrases as though he were addressing a crowd.

The establishment, for lack of a better word, was, by today's standards, overtly reactionary in the early and mid-sixties. When I graduated nothing had really changed, nor would it for the next few years. There was no meaningful dialogue between the administration and students on any issue whatsoever and this widened the generation gap, which was already a Grand Canyon to begin with.

The Rolling Stones came along after the Beatles,

and "I Can't Get No Satisfaction," written by Mick Jagger and Keith Richards, was released in early June, 1965. It busted things wide open. Richard's aggressive riffs at the beginning, followed by Jagger's howling protest echoed the frustration and angst of an entire generation that would become increasingly more outspoken in its rejection of traditional values. The Stones, of course, were more than satisfied with the record sales and weren't about to change their style.

I'd been hanging out with a new group of guys who made a conscious effort of defying rules and regulations. The jocks I used to hang out with were disappointing. I mean they weren't too swift.

One evening me and Ray and Zeek went cruising in the suburbs. Zeek pulled the car over in a street where there was no traffic and lit a joint. They didn't say anything, but I knew it was marijuana because of the smell. They took a couple of hits then passed it to me. I smoked it like a cigarette and said I didn't feel anything. So Ray told me to hold the smoke in my lungs longer, which I did. After that I was sailing in a world of euphoria, of well-being. I had probably never felt so good before. The music on the car radio suddenly became different. It had greater depth and actually seemed to be coming from every direction. I could hear the different musicians with greater clarity.

It was as if the sound had become palpable, as though you could touch it and see it. Figures were being projected from the music in a way that some would describe as hallucinatory. The dimensions of time and space were changed, too. Time was slowed down immensely and the song on the radio–I think it was the latest hit by the Supremes–seemed to go on forever and ever without end.

I'm not usually very talkative, but after smoking the joint, I became a virtual chatterbox, describing my sensations, my impressions and who I thought I was. Zeek was so annoyed he simply told me to shut up.

All in all, the marijuana made me feel euphoric, something that alcohol had never been able to do before. While excessive use of alcohol could make me sick or belligerent, the grass made me sociable and amiable. It made me want to open up and understand my surroundings.

We smoked another joint of Mexican weed and went cruising around the suburbs. I just stretched out in the back seat of the Pontiac and enjoyed the music and the new sensations. Afterwards I could say that grass usually made me feel good, but I'd never felt exactly the way I felt the first time I smoked. I suppose that was due to the uniqueness of the experience.

When I got home, there was not much for me to do,

so I just went to bed and crashed.

15

2

Getting Illegal

My first toke on a reefer made me a virtual criminal. Was I worried about that? Well, to be honest, I didn't feel immediately threatened by that euphoric toke, but somewhere in the back of my mind I realized there was potential danger. Of course I wasn't a dealer or anything, and maybe I felt somewhat reassured by the fact that more and more people were smoking dope and that it was subtly being advertised by rock bands and celebrities. Those who were in favor of legalizing or at least decriminalizing pot, were *avant-garde* and cool, while those who were opposed to it were right-wingers, reactionaries or outright fascists.

How many young people were smoking dope in 1965? There are no reliable statistics on the subject, but in my town at that time, I would guess that one in seven or one in eight had smoked dope, and that number was increasing exponentially. Even the most unlikely people were turning on in high school, like sports queens and student presidents. We knew that some teachers smoked dope, especially the ones from Berkeley, but, of course, they could never admit it publicly. There was a counselor, though, whose name was Jerry, who was pretty cool, and we knew that he smoked grass, but he was careful not to talk about it, because his job was on the line, and he had a family of three kids and rent to pay.

Allen Ginsberg, the poet, made us laugh when he admitted in his poem "America" that he smoked marijuana every chance he got. That wasn't just a line in the poem, oh no! That was the truth. Rock music at the time made allusions to smoking dope with words like "high" and "getting stoned," and the mainstream radio stations banned certain records or forced groups to change the lyrics or mumble the key words so the songs would be acceptable for wholesome American youth who ate Wonder Bread and said their prayers when they went to bed. But we knew what was going on. We knew that the Beatles and the Stones smoked weed and that San Francisco bands like Jefferson Airplane, the Grateful Dead and Big Brother and the Holding Company got high and not just on grass. Shit, we weren't stupid.

We knew that Bob Dylan turned the Beatles on to dope, too. He didn't win any medals for that, but he did receive quite a bit of notoriety in the counterculture. It all happened at the Hotel Delmonico where you had to be a celebrity to get through the lines of cops to reach the Beatles' suite. To tell the truth, Bobby was not that hot on the Fab Four, whom he referred to as "Bubblegum." But not everyone I knew liked Robert Zimmerman's whiny voice or shitty attitude either.

Timothy Leary, high priest of the psychedelic counterculture, was about as candid as you could get about getting high. For Leary and his acolytes, smoking weed or using psychedelic drugs was a religion, and as such, getting high was a right guaranteed by the First Amendment of the Constitution.

Doctor Leary had long been designated by the establishment as an extremely dangerous man, or even the most dangerous man in the country. Those of us in our teens laughed at this without understanding the extreme duress that it caused for the Harvard professor who had to be considered one of the most brilliant professors in his field of study.

In the fall of 1965 at Millbrook, New York, Tim was living his happy days with Rosemary, his good looking companion. They spent their time making love in the alcove ceilinged with mirrors, going on picnics by the lake, or for long, leisurely walks on the gorgeous estate, seeking hidden streams or woods, becoming one with nature, smoking good grass, working in their garden, or laughing with candid innocence as they gyrated to the latest rock 'n' roll hits. Yet sinister spies sent by the local sheriff sought to infiltrate the Millbrook. Happy days were soon to end, though the former Harvard professor and his charming companion were too busy editing books and preparing slide shows for their psychedelic workshops to notice the sinister forces mounting against them. But it was clear that the Feds wanted to bust the LSD guru, and soon bogus telephone repairmen were showing up unexpectedly to check the wires or something else. Word was out that the district attorney from Poughkeepsie was busily organizing a raid, maybe because panties were being dropped faster than the acid in Millbrook. Oh!

Amidst growing pressure, Tim announced he was closing the estate and heading south of the border to Mexico. Leary, always a bestseller, was promised a handsome advance for an autobiographical work. With Rosemary, his daughter Susan and his friend Jack, they hit the road *en route* to Mexico. But clouds kept them from going over the psychedelic rainbow. The group was prohibited from entering Mexico at the Laredo crossing for administrative reasons, so he headed back to the United States, which turned out to be a huge mistake, since Nuevo Laredo is classified as a *free zone*, so they could have taken a room at a hotel and returned to the immigration office the next day. Tim wondered if anybody was holding grass. He should have thought about that before, but Tim's parents gave him a really bad script for life. Jack flushed his weed down the toilet, but Rosemary was unable to get rid of the small amount of grass she had in a silver box, and that mess-up proved to be their undoing. At the American border, a customs agent immediately found a seed that he supposed was marijuana, and the station wagon was surrounded by agents who ordered the vehicle to be emptied of all baggage. It didn't take long to find the weed, and bail was set for a whopping $100,000. Like clockwork, a group of US investigators and prosecutors was dispatched to the scene. "We've got the son of a bitch!" they must have said. Although the small quantity of grass was found on Susan, Tim said he'd take responsibility for it, which meant he was charged with three felonies. Later, the court sentenced Tim to thirty years in prison and a $40,000 fine for less than an ounce of marijuana. That was America's idea of justice at the time. His daughter Susan was sentenced to a period of five years. Of course we were all thoroughly shocked by the absurd severity of the sentence, and many celebrities signed a petition of support, including Steve Allen, Peter Fonda, Jules Feiffer, Norman Mailer,

Anaïs Nin and others.

What effect did Tim's ordeal have on young people like myself? We could see that this was a clear case of harassment. We knew that the older generation had lied about marijuana for years, and we wanted it to be legalized. Our parents, except for a few happy exceptions, were against legalization, despite the fact that they knew nothing about weed and had never smoked grass. We were pretty sure that if they had, they wouldn't have been so uptight about it. But they didn't know jack about it.

The laws prohibiting the use of marijuana go back a long way, and the truth of the matter is that they were basically racist in nature. After the long and bloody Mexican Revolution, Mexicans began emigrating and crossed the southern border in the early 1920s to live in the United States. They had a history of smoking "marijuana," the Mexican word for cannabis, and they continued to smoke and cultivate weed once they lived in the USA.

Weed made its way into the black ghettoes and big cities via ports like New Orleans. At that time, it was mostly associated with Mexicans or jazz musicians, but that didn't stop some people in the Hollywood film industry from smoking it. Jazz musicians liked to smoke grass because it helped them to play better; and then Cab Calloway and his orchestra recorded "The Reefer Man" in 1932. It's certainly no coincidence that the final draft of The Uniform Narcotic Drug Act was adopted in the same year, arduously promoted by Harry J. Anslinger, anti-marijuana evangelist and head of the Federal Bureau of Narcotics, whose prolonged campaign of disinformation and bigotry helped to demonize cannabis in America. Anslinger seemed to have a particular animosity towards blacks and musicians, and kept a special file on well-known singers like Billie Holiday, whom he was bent on getting prosecuted. Some have said he was responsible, at least in part, for her death.

The basic and unproven claim by Anslinger was that cannabis was responsible for crime, violence and moral deprivation. J. Edgar Hoover of the Federal Bureau of Investigation said pretty much the same thing, claiming that reefers were responsible for "murder, assault, rape, physical demoralization and mental breakdown." None of these claims were based on fact, and, of course, none of the anti-marijuana zealots had ever smoked weed, so they didn't know what they were talking about. But often being at the head of a powerful government bureau is all it takes to control public opinion.

In the mid-sixties things weren't any different. The

high school authorities echoed the sermons of the establishment in general and the local school board in particular, but we weren't duped. We knew—you could tell by the way they dressed, the way they talked and the way they combed their hair—they didn't know what they were talking about. Virtually everyone who was down on marijuana had never smoked a joint; those who had knew that the school officials were full of shit.

The press was quick to jump on the band wagon because it sold newspapers. Generic articles liked to whip up racial prejudice by saying crime in the Southwest United States was linked to smoking pot by Mexican-Americans and/or illegal aliens sneaking across the Rio Grande. Some asserted that the insidious drug traffic was a result of unchecked immigration and that degenerate dope pushers were giving away joints to minors. Other lurid tales described how marijuana was being used to seduce virgins, who, because of their innocence, were easy prey to the morally depraved drug peddlers. That was the kind of bullshit they were dishing out.

Many Americans in the twenties and thirties learned about marijuana by reading William Randolf Hearst's tabloids, whose titles used words like "bloodlust" or "killer weed," and said normal individuals were being transformed into depraved "fiends" of all shapes and sizes. His papers also fueled racial stereotypes of Negroes with horrendous tales of voodoo jazz and sexual assault.

Movies have always been a convenient means of propaganda, and not only in dictatorships, and there were a number of films warning against the evils of marijuana. One evening when I was in the City looking for dope, I decided to go see *Reefer Madness*, a 1936 low budget film that had become a self-parody in the sixties, particularly in San Francisco because of the bourgeoning Haight-Ashbury. We baby boomers didn't take the film seriously, but there were still some geezers in the older generation who did, or at least seemed to. The events of the story were blown up out of all proportion, to say the least, and that was because the producers hoped to scare parents and at least some adolescents out of their wits. In the film, high school students are enticed by marijuana dealers to smoke a few joints, and that leads to a hit and run accident, death of a pedestrian, suicide, conspiracy to commit murder, attempted rape and insanity; and all that because of a few joints. It was pure nonsense.

When I walked into the Times movie theater, the film had already begun. Inside the house there was a buzz in the air and a thick layer of smoke above the movie goers. You could see the joints lighting up as people took hits, and the smell of marijuana was strong enough to knock you over. You could get a contact high just by being in the theater.

When the movie began, the spectators got carried away and screeched with gales of laughter, hissed, heckled or booed the actors as one would traditionally do with a melodrama. When the high school principal came on at the end of the film to warn parents about the dangers of marijuana and began pointing his finger, the audience became riotous. Some threw their empty popcorn boxes at the screen, and somebody threw what appeared to be underwear, although I can't confirm this. A few told him to shut his trap, turn on and drop out.

Of course there were other ridiculous movies used to spread propaganda like *She Shoulda Said 'No'!* Their premises were essentially the same: marijuana would change a normal person into a criminal, a murderer, a rapist and a lunatic. The officials where I went to high school had the dumb idea of showing students one of these films during a general assembly. I forget what the name was, but it didn't get very far. We all knew why we'd been assembled and the general feeling was that we were not going to be treated like sheep. During the first moments of the film, when the credits were being shown, a monotonous and driving beat was played. Spontaneously, and without the slightest cue, the three hundred students assembled began clapping their hands and stamping their feet to satirize the film. This went on for about three minutes before the principal, Mr. Merrytown, became irate, turned on the lights and said: "I see that you are already too far gone, and that there is no point in trying to *educate* you. Please leave now!" Believe me, there was a lot of laughter and a dash of vulgarity, too. And, so, that's what we did. Everyone filed out of the auditorium, clapping their hands rhythmically and chanting "Merry-Town is a clown!" At least half of us took the principal's bidding as an invitation to cut classes for the rest of the day, and we were out the door and up into the nearest canyon smoking grass and having fun.

Was grass easier to get in the fifties? I don't think so, because there was probably less demand for it. In 1965 it wasn't always that easy to come by. Some adventurous souls drove across the southern border to Tiahuana, but a few of them got ripped off, to say the least. Either the weed was bad or they got robbed. Some, however, knew how to go about it, and they could score as many keys as they could afford and then drive back across the border when it was safe. Of course, there was always the chance of getting busted, so you had to know how to play the game.

3

Scoring Weed

Scoring weed in the sixties was one huge hassle. You had to have a connection and because of the pressure from police and the establishment, suspicion was rampant. In many ways, there seemed to be bigger risks in the suburbs where narks had an easier job of finding out who was dealing what. When they were pretty sure of what somebody was doing, they would try to set them up so they would have evidence to use against them in court. When a bust was made, they would have leverage against that person and would try to get him to stool on others, so they could make as many arrests as possible. I don't remember hearing of any girls or women selling drugs, but I wasn't that interested in that aspect of it.

There was this one dude–Bobby G–whose name frequently came up when the conversation was about dope. I never bought any drugs from him, but it was widely known that he was dealing grass and other stuff like heroin. His mother, a very thin and nervous person, was supposedly an addict, so maybe that's what got him interested in drugs. There was something about Bobby that stuck in my mind, something in his face, his eyes and his arrogant attitude that told me he was not to be trusted; so I never asked him if he was holding anything. Besides, I wanted my pot smoking to be as anonymous as possible, and in the suburbs, where everyone pretty much knew everyone else, word about drug users got around fast.

People and the media were talking more and more about the Haight-Ashbury in San Francisco, so I figured that was probably a good place to go looking for weed. I had an old Ford pickup truck at the time, not the best wheels to go cruising, but I got it cheap and the motor was reliable, and so one Saturday I made sure I had plenty of gas in the tank and drove over the Bay Bridge to check things out. And that day I hit a hole in one.

I parked my pickup on Waller Street, walked up to Haight Street in the Fillmore district–maybe a little risky at the time, but there weren't any hassles–and then headed for Buena Vista Park, one of my favorite places. As I got near Haight and Masonic, I started looking around to see if anybody was dealing. There were no cops in sight, so I felt reassured. I got as far as Stanyon and couldn't see anything happening, so I turned around and headed back towards Haight and Ashbury. It was thereabouts that three guys in their early twenties who looked like college students, with fairly long hair and mustaches, asked me if I wanted some grass. These were certainly no smelly, barefoot hippies described by Mister Boraxo. They were dressed casually, but neatly.

I said, "Yeah, show me what you got." So one of them took out an ounce and opened the baggy. I looked at the weed and took a whiff. "Wow, that smells really good. Why is the grass red?"

"Hey, man, do you know what this is? This is Panama Red!"

"Panama Red? I don't think I've ever smoked any of that."

"Say, man, this weed is really groovy. Like it's a real trip, man."

"Far out. Ok, how much is it?"

"Ten bucks."

"Ok, I'll take one."

I handed him the money and put what looked like a full ounce in my coat pocket. They smiled and told me to enjoy it, and that I did.

With time to burn and a little money in my pocket, I decided to go see Frances, a girl I knew in the City. Now she didn't live in the Haight or any cheap neighborhood, oh no! She lived in a ritzy apartment in

Pacific Heights. I met her at a Jefferson Airplane concert at Fillmore Auditorium. She liked psychedelic music and loved to smoke good grass, so I was pretty sure she would like to try some Panama Red and listen to some groovy music on her expensive stereo equipment. I called her up from a nearby phone booth and she told me to come over, saying that her roommate, an airline stewardess, was not around. I liked to walk in San Francisco and the busses and cable cars were usually crowded on Saturdays, so I just walked up Masonic Avenue and then Presidio to get to Pacific Heights.

When I got to her place, I rang the buzzer and waited for her to come. After a moment, she opened the door, smiled and gestured for me to come in. We went upstairs and sat on an expensive sofa and got into some small talk, with her asking what brought me to the City. I told her I had come to score some grass and took out the lid I bought on Haight Street. I opened up the baggie so she could smell it and see what the grass was like.

"I don't think I've ever seen grass this color, and it smells really strong," she said.

"Yeah, neither have I. The guys that sold it to me said it's *Panama Red*. So I guess it comes from Panama. Say, do you have any rolling papers?"

"Sure!"

She came back with the ZigZags and turned on *Rubber Soul* while I rolled a super bomber. Her choice of records was good, because *Rubber Soul* was the Beatles' pot album, so to speak, since they were smoking weed when they made it, though not necessarily during the recording sessions because the tapes were shitty when they were *too* high. By the time *Revolver* was produced, they had all dropped acid, including Paul, the last one to do so.

When John was singing the first bars of "Norwegian Wood," we were in a totally different space, and the music seemed to be coming from every direction: up, down, north, south, east, west, inside and outside. I leaned back on the sofa and started laughing for no particular reason, except that I felt good. Frances, who had made some tea somehow, came back into the room and put it on the coffee table. I passed her the joint that was burning really well and she took another hit. She sat down on the sofa and began singing along with the Beatles. We played records for the rest of the afternoon and then her telephone rang. It was her roommate telling Frances she came back earlier than expected, and that she was taking a taxi to the apartment. That put Frances in a blue funk. I could see the sirens going off in her head. She said we had to air the room because her roommate was *really* straight and hated marijuana and everything associated with it, so we scrambled to get rid of the smoke and hide the pungent smell of grass by opening all the windows and spraying the room with air freshener.

I stuck around for a while and met Frances's roommate and her mainstream mind. She sipped her bourbon on the rocks and gave her opinions on Vietnam and the red menace. Apparently she didn't smell the weed because she didn't say anything. There was no point in my hanging around because the party was over. I asked Frances if she wanted to see a Jefferson Airplane concert at the Fillmore that evening and she said that sounded good and suggested we meet outside the Fillmore.

Outside the music venue I saw Frances coming down the street and I waved to let her know I'd already arrived. We walked up the stairs inside to get our tickets and Frances reached into the barrel to take a free apple, which she took a small bite from and then held it up to my face for me to take a bite, which I did.

There was a thick layer of smoke inside the dance hall and you could see young people lighting up in the corners of the room. When Bill Graham introduced the original Airplane comprised of Marty Balin, Signe

Anderson, Jorma Kaukonen, Paul Kantner, Jack Casady and Skip Spence, the band came on stage and the Airplane took off. The audience applauded the way you do when you're really stoned. Jefferson Airplane sang their usual repertoire including "The Other Side of This Life," "Let's Get Together" and "It's No Secret." It was a nice evening, but it was starting to get cloaked in smoke. I remember lying on the floor and kissing Frances before everything became cloudy. I walked her to her apartment and then drove my pickup back home. It must have been well after two in the morning when I finally got into town, but not wishing to go to bed right away, I stopped off at an all-night restaurant to have something to eat. The place was crowded because of the bar rush, but I found a seat at the counter and ordered a breakfast steak with hash brown potatoes. When I finished, I drove home and crashed without waking my parents.

For a while the Haight-Ashbury was my most reliable place for scoring weed. What I usually did was take Highway 880 to Oakland and then cross the Bay Bridge to San Francisco. Of course there were times when I came up empty handed, or paranoia got the best of me when there were too many police patrolling in the street. There were so-called plainclothes cops, too, but they were pretty conspicuous it seemed to me and the

Psychedelic Shop posted pictures of them in its window, which made the Thelins *really* popular with the local heat.

One time I saw this long-haired dude openly dealing grass in the street, so I figured I could hit on him. I waited until he finished his transaction with another guy before asking him if he had any lids to sell. Now this dude was *really* far out. I was wondering where he bought his crazy clothes, because you would never find them at Sears and Roebuck or Montgomery Ward. As naturally as you could imagine, he was standing there on Haight Street wearing black and white striped pants, a top hat, a fluorescent yellow shirt with bright red stars, an Afghan vest and pink felt Beatle boots.

"Say, man," I said, approaching him. "I can dig your groovy apparel. What about weed, man. Sellin' any smoke?"

"Cool, man. Like, what's your trip?"

"Just some groovy grass, if you have any."

From there on out it was easy. He told me he didn't have any more lids on him, so we'd have to go back to his place on Masonic. I followed him to his room. The vibes were good, so I didn't fear a rip-off or anything. His room was what you might call a typical hippy pad, no derogatory connotations implied. He lived in one room which he used for sleeping, smoking and dealing pot. There was a naked mattress on the floor with pillows used for chairs. Indian blankets of various colors covered the walls and ceiling. On a small coffee table was a hookah with a jar of grass. There were no windows.

Without asking any questions, he loaded the pipe and lit it for us to smoke; he also lit some rose-scented incense that was very fragrant and helped to hide the smell of grass. He turned on some Indian raga that we listened to as we smoked the weed that was pungent and strong. In a very short time I felt really stoned. We rapped about this and that. He said he was from Pittsburgh and that he'd come to Frisco to escape the draft. I told him that I was living in the suburbs, that I liked the City and that I came to the Haight from time to time to score some weed. "I've changed my name since I've moved to the Haight to begin a new existence. You can call me Shah Noorani, or just plain Shah," he said.

"Yeah, ok," I replied. "And you can just call me Lou, or Bert, whichever you prefer."

Shah took another stick of incense out of a drawer and lit it. Then he placed the *I Ching* on the rug, took six sticks and carefully rolled them in the palm of his hand before religiously spreading them out on the floor. He looked knowingly at the lines that were formed and said, "That's interesting. It's hexagram seven, the army." Then he opened the *I Ching* to the corresponding page and read: "One must fight enthusiastically to overcome obstacles in order to achieve a just goal." Next he opened another drawer of the dresser and took out a lid of grass. "Would you like to smoke a joint to see what my grass is like?" he asked. I told him that was a good idea. "Do you like Indian raga," he asked, holding a Ravi Shankar LP in one hand for me to see. I said that was fine with me. He put it on the turntable and modulated the volume.

The grass was good and the Indian music put me on a different plane. As we listened to the music and smoked the weed, Shah began quoting from the *Tao Teh King*. "To those who are good (to me), I am good; and to those who are not good (to me), I am also good; and thus (all) get to be good. To those who are sincere (with me), I am sincere; and to those who are not sincere (with me), I am also sincere; and thus (all) get to be sincere."

He said the lid was $10, the going rate in the Haight, and that I could drop by whenever I wanted to score some groovy grass. I thanked him for his laid-back attitude and got ready to drive back to the East Bay and enjoy my acquisition.

There were times when there was nothing happening on Haight Street, for whatever reason. I did my best to avoid the *rush hour* on weekends, because that was just a big hassle. One day I saw this hippy girl wearing lots of jewelry, dressed in Salvation Army glory, and asked if she lived in the neighborhood. When she said she did, I asked her where she thought I could score a lid. She said I should try Hippie Hill in Golden Gate Park.

"Hippie Hill?" I asked.

"Yeah, it's not that far from the Panhandle. Just go up Fell Street and into the Park on John F. Kennedy Drive. You'll see it to your left," she said with a flower child smile.

"That's cool," I replied and thanked her for the tip.

I found the spacious meadow between Kezar Drive and Kennedy Drive and started walking in a leisurely pace towards a group of young people who were sitting in a group. When the wind blew my way I got a good whiff of weed. Ensconced in Golden Gate Park the Hippie Hill enclave was considered off limits to straights and police. There were dogs running around, people playing with a Frisbee or flying a kite or just rolling in the grass to have fun. Others were sitting in groups, playing the guitar or bongos. The vibrations were good and there were no cops in sight. I just sat down close to the group as though I belonged there.

They were burning sweet-smelling incense and sharing apples and oranges. There was a lot of laughter and I could see a guy taking a hit off a joint and passing it to the person next to him. It wasn't long before a girl not far from me smiled and held out a joint for me to take. I took a couple of hits off it before passing it to someone else. The mellow atmosphere made communication easy, and so I asked this girl if she knew where I could score some good grass. She said that was no problem and pointed to a guy with a colorful Mexican serape, sandals and a headband.

"Say man, I can dig your serape. Ya know, I'd really like to score some grass," I said, as I approached him.

"No problemo, hombre," he said with a stoner voice. "How much do you want?"

"Oh, just a lid."

He reached under his serape, a way of concealing his wares, took out a bulging baggie and handed it to me. I opened the lid to smell the weed, and then asked him how much. He said it was $10. I handed him the Hamilton and said "We the People thank you."

"Right on, man. Enjoy the smoke."

I stayed with this group for a while. We spoke about the local music scene, the heat coming down on brothers and sisters in the Haight, and how to make really good Alice B. Toklas brownies. They asked where I was from, and I said I was from the suburbs, where the heat was really uptight. When I told them I sometimes scored grass on Haight Street, they told me you had to be careful, because undercover cops dressed like hippies were taking pictures of dealers in the street, and that they were probably using them as evidence. I thanked them for the information and left Hippie Hill and San Francisco feeling high.

The Psychedelic Shop at 1535 Haight Street was a well-known paraphernalia shop owned by Ron and Jay Thelin, where you could buy records, occult books, incense, jewelry, posters, rolling papers, tickets to dance concerts and sometimes more. I had heard on the street that if you were cool and knew how to ask for it, you could score.

I walked in one day in early March 1966, when there weren't too many customers, leafed through *The Tibetan Book of the Dead* and then picked up some rose scented incense. I don't know who was running the store that day, but he seemed pretty hip and mellow. I asked for some ZigZag rolling papers, hinting that it would be really groovy to have some "tea" to get turned on. The guy smiled to himself, reached under the counter and put a baggie in front of me, which I promptly put in my pants. I paid for my merchandise, told the guy he had a heavy shop and went joyfully out the front door.

Ronald Reagan, the ex-movie star and glib apologist for the Republican Party, had been forcefully campaigning for the governorship of California. Roaring for law and order, he criticized the myth of the Great Society, declared he would limit government spending, lower taxes, "clean up the mess at Berkeley," fight obscenity and restore capital punishment. The counterculture of the Haight-Ashbury knew what to expect from a conservative crusader who cited the examples of Jackie Robinson and Willy Mays as proof of racial integration. Mr. Boraxo won the election against Pat Brown on 8 November 1966 by a landslide, capturing 57.5% of the votes, and, it could be added, without the help of Ken Kesey, who was planning on dosing the Democrats. After the election, things started changing right away, and not just at U. C. Berkeley, home of the Free Speech Movement. The Psychedelic Shop was raided by the San Francisco police for obscenity. Lenore Kandel's short book of poems, *The Love Book*, was seized by police, and Allen Cohen, editor of *The San Francisco Oracle*, was arrested. He happened to be working behind the counter that day.

As it so happens, I had decided to drop into the shop,

but saw a message posted on the front door saying it was closed because of the bust. Was it all about obscenity? If you're interested the word comes from the Latin *obscenus*, meaning disgusting to the senses, abhorrent to morality or virtue, attempting to incite lust or depravity. If one took those meanings into account, the streets of North Beach should immediately have come under scrutiny because of the hardcore papers on the public newsstands depicting fornication, fellatio or cunnilingus. But since organized crime had a lot of sway in city politics, and because pornography was controlled largely by the mafia, the local authorities in San Francisco ignored it. Besides, pornography was the bread and butter of the nightclubs on Broadway, and that brought in a lot of tourist money. In truth, the bust was not about pornography at all, but about harassing The Psychedelic Shop and the *Oracle*, which printed articles about police brutality. If the hippies of the Haight were not paranoid, they had plenty of reasons to be, because the formidable forces of the federal, state and local governments were being mobilized to nip flower power in the bud.

Two days before Thanksgiving at the Poetry Center on the San Francisco State campus, a group of professors at the college decided to fight back and protest against obscenity laws by reading *The Love*

Book and a selection of passages from Michael McClure's play *The Beard*, which had also been censored. Although their publicized reading was in part intended to be a provocation, local authorities did not interrupt the reading attended by three hundred enthusiastic people.

Kandel's short book of erotic poems was judged obscene in 1967, but the ruling was fortunately overturned by a higher court as a violation of First Amendment rights to freedom of expression. Most people in the Haight considered the affair to be nothing more than cultural bias against the counterculture, and many personalities in the neighborhood, like Allen Cohen of *The San Francisco Oracle*, were outspoken about it. Cohen wondered what stance to take with a court that apparently had an axe to grind. Perhaps trying to look respectable, as far as the court's perception of the word was concerned, he wore a white shirt and tied his hair back in a tight ponytail, but he kept his sandals and hippie beads.

For the counterculture the establishment's attitude reeked of fascism and Puritanism. Certainly totalitarian regimes have always sought to control thought by restricting print and other forms of communication, but revolutionary America stood for freedom of thought and expression. That the arresting officers saw *The*

Love Book as hard core pornography proves how little they knew about Kandel's poems or about poetry in general. They did not know why the book was created and what it was for. People in the counterculture read *The Love Book* as a celebration of sexual union between a man and a woman and not as something shameful or pornographic.

One of the truly remarkable coffeehouses in the neighborhood was the Blue Unicorn, at 1927 Hayes Street, just a block away from the Panhandle. The coffeehouse was a little cramped inside because it was roughly twice as long as it was wide, but it was still a good place to go. Like its clientele, it was anything but luxurious: the tables and chairs were flimsy, like the small booths in the back. There was graffiti everywhere, and customers added to it all the time. The ceiling was far out and difficult to describe because it was so heterogeneous, with psychedelic colors, expressions and motifs everywhere and extending in all directions. The Blue Unicorn was a regular hangout for poets, Diggers and rock bands.

I walked in one evening and managed to find a seat at a table that had one leg shorter than the others. The place was pretty dark because the only lighting there were the candles on the tables. I guess they were trying to save electricity or something. One guy was playing with Tarot cards, another seemed to be crashed out, with his head on the table, another was covered in all kinds of hippie beads and jewelry, while still another looked like he was impersonating Jesus Christ. I ordered a cup of coffee and checked out the scene. Barry McGuire's "Eve of Destruction" was playing on the radio.

The smell of marijuana was coming from one of the booths in the back and joints were lighting up when this couple took hits. If their laughter was any indication, they must have been in a really good mood. I decided to test my luck, getting up slowly and walking to the back of the place. "Say, that smells really groovy. I sure would like to get stoned."

They gave me the once over, trying to decide if I was safe or not. I think they could see I wasn't a narc, so they invited me to sit down with them, which I did. The guy took out a stash and began to roll a joint. When he finished he handed it to me. I used the candle on the table to light the doobie and took a hit.

"Say, man, this tastes really good. What is it?" I asked.

"Can ya dig it? This is Acapulco Gold. It's a sativa strain that comes from around Acapulco," he said.

"Groovy, man. I can feel it already. Say, if you've

got a lid to spare, I could dig it."

"Sure, no problem."

He reached into his coat pocket, took out a plastic baggie and handed it to me. I took a Hamilton out of my wallet and held it out to him, without asking the price. He just took the money and gave it to the hippie girl sitting next to him. She smiled and put it in her pocket.

"Ever drop any acid, man?" he asked.

"Uh, no. Can't say that I have."

"I've got some really groovy Owsley if you want to score," he said.

I hesitated before answering. He held out what looked like a small white pill, and added: "This is White Lightning, man, a really heavy trip. And it's pure lysergic acid; it hasn't been cut with anything else, like speed."

"How much a hit?"

"Two-fifty," he said.

I took five bucks out of my pocket and handed it to him and he gave me two tabs.

"It's a good idea to take it with friends, people with good vibes, and best to drop it in the country or in a comfortable place where you feel good, like in the Park. That way you'll have a good trip. Don't take it with people who are uptight. That's a bummer."

As far as I can remember, I followed his advice.

4

Native Americans

The American Indians were the original Native Americans in North America. The adventurous spirits who dared to penetrate the foreign territory within the continental limits of the United States of America on tour busses could not help but notice the number of hippies dressed up as Indians. There is a special reason for this, of course, it's because the Native Americans occupied a special place in the psychedelic counterculture.

The cactus peyote played a part in that identification, of which more can be said later, but there were basic social and cultural reasons that draw our immediate attention. But what was it about the American Indians that so fascinated the hippies, to such an extent that many sought to emulate their more ostensible characteristics?

If the hippies felt a strong kinship with the American Indians, it was in part because of peyote. The Native Americans religiously used the cactus in their sacred ceremonies because of the mescaline in it, a psychoactive substance within the peyote buttons capable of inducing altered states of consciousness, similar to the hallucinatory effects of lysergic acid diethylamide. The Native Americans turned on, like the hippies of the Haight-Ashbury, to meet the Great Spirit. For some tribes peyote was a sacrament, and a pathway to the Eternal. As with all laws regarding drugs, the use of peyote as a controlled substance is, with regards to federal law, complicated. However, American Indians are allowed by law to use it in their ceremonials. Similarly, many hippies in the Haight felt that they should be allowed to use LSD for *religious* purposes. With the International Federation for Internal Freedom (IFIF) and the League for Spiritual Discovery (LSD), Timothy Leary adamantly advocated the use of lysergic acid diethylamide for religious purposes, like the Native Americans. So, from the very beginning, the counterculture felt a strong kinship with Indians as far as religion and drugs were concerned.

I met a girl at the I/Thou coffee shop that had a lot to say about Indians. In fact, she was dressed like an American Indian, with doeskin moccasins, an elaborate suede jacket with fringe, a peacock feather headband and a lot of turquoise jewelry. She was sitting alone so I asked if I could join her and offered to fill up her coffee cup. I said I liked her Indian getup and asked her about it. She seemed eager to talk and began a monologue.

"Did you know that the American Indians were the *only real* Native Americans? Many inhabited the North American continent for tens of thousands of years before they were exterminated by Europeans; the first exterminator was Christopher Columbus. People in the Haight-Ashbury feel very strongly about our kinship with Indians. Like African-Americans and the freaks of Hashbury, they have always been an oppressed people. That's why we identify with them. And you know, anyone can be a Native American if they adopt the values of those cultures which, unlike the white man's civilization, live in harmony with the environment. Growing up in this country we were all fed the propaganda on television about white culture with the westerns and stories about cowboys and Indians. The Indians were always seen as bloodthirsty savages craving to add new scalps to their collections. The cowboys and settlers were always the good guys; the Indians were always the bad guys: a classic Manichaean melodrama. I'm wearing these clothes because I've adopted the attitudes of the American Indians. If you look around here, you'll see there are quite a few people like me. That's why so many of us are wearing headbands. I've changed my name, too. My name is

Golden Dawn. I've become a completely new person since I've moved to the Haight-Ashbury and dropped acid. In a very real sense I've been reborn. If you'd have seen me just twelve months ago, you'd never have recognized me. It all came to me in an acid trip. I've taken mescaline and peyote, too, but acid turned me on to my true nature, to who I *really* am. LSD soon became my sacrament. Like the Indians, some of us have formed "tribes" that we call communes, because we believe that communal living is more natural, a more humane way of living. There are several communes here in the neighborhood and many more in the country. I'm living here now, but someday I'll move out to the country to get back to nature; but I'd like to do it with the right people. The Native Americans, unlike white culture, lived off the land. They had a profound spiritual awareness of nature and communicated with the Great Spirit everywhere. They didn't have to go into a church to worship because the landscape was their church. Many of the freaks here feel they were Indians in another life and that they've been reincarnated. That's why they revere Indians so much. Like Dr. Leary said, this time around you can be whoever you want to be. You don't have to buy into consumer culture, go to college, work nine to five, and try to keep up with the Joneses. I know that a lot of people in the establishment laugh at us, but they all have the wrong dreams. We're not capitalists and not the slaves of our government or our parents. I'm freer today than I've ever been and it's because I've dropped out of the mainstream that has nothing worthwhile to offer. White culture is only concerned with exploiting other people. It stole Native American lands, broke treaties, destroyed Indian culture and massacred tribes everywhere. I don't want to have anything to do with a culture that steals, murders and plunders everywhere it goes. That's what it's done to Negroes, too."

I thanked Golden Dawn for telling me so much about the American Indians. We drank another cup of coffee, and then she left with a long-haired dude who smelled of patchouli.

The profound respect and admiration felt by freaks in the Haight for Indians is perhaps best exemplified by *The San Francisco Oracle – The Psychedelic Newspaper of the Haight Ashbury*, conceived by the visionary Allen Cohen. The eighth publication of the rainbow tabloid was entitled "The American Indian." It's one of the best issues of the *Oracle* with numerous articles of varying significance: "Tu Wa Qa Chi: The Fourth World," "Sunbear Speaks," "Kiva," "Living with the Land," "Indians for Sale," "Who Is an Indian,"

"Sioux Songs," "Hopi Life Plan," "Indians, Herbs & Religion," plus poems by Gary Snyder, Bob Kaufman and Philip Lamantha, "Psychedelic Yoga," letters to the editor and the habitual want ads that always said so much about the psychedelic culture of the Haight-Ashbury.

The poster art and drawings by Wes Wilson, Stanley "Mouse" Miller, and Rick Griffin say a lot about the revolution in San Francisco that is spreading across the land. Most of these original posters were produced for Chet Helms of the Family Dog and Bill Graham. Wes's poster for the Family Dog in 1966, depicting a Native American in a top hat smoking a reefer, with a different form of the Stars and Stripes in the background, and the ironic aphorism in the form of a legend on his chest, is a classic of Haight-Ashbury poster art. Helms gave Wilson the photograph of the American Indian wearing a top hat and smoking a long pipe. It was taken from the *American Heritage Book of Indians* and used to create the logo for the Family Dog, together with the epigrammatic witticism "May the baby Jesus shut your mouth and open your mind." The highly unusual depiction, although seemingly derogatory, was in fact meant to show the wisdom of the Native Americans who rejected mainstream values while enjoying the sacrament of the psychedelic counterculture. Like so many young people in the Haight, he, too, seemed to be wearing a costume.

55

4

Groovin' at the Love Pageant Rally

The Albin Rooming House, 1090 Page Street, San Francisco, September 1966.

Peter and Rodney Albin rented cheap rooms to students at San Francisco State, where the two folkies were also enrolled. The big house had a groovy basement with all kinds of luxurious stuff like wood panels and a stage. Their buddy Chet Helms used it as a ballroom for the out of sight jams he organized. Big Brother and the Holding Company, Quicksilver Messenger Service and Sopwith Camel were created from the gigs there.

Zizi and Cheetah (not their real names) were smoking dope and grooving to the Stones when, for some unknown reason, Cheetah decided to look out the bedroom window. He saw two cops writing down license plate numbers of parked cars. This made Cheetah really uptight. Zizi could see that his roommate was pissed off about something and asked why he was freaking out.

"Shit man, there's these two pigs in the street snooping around," said Cheetah.

"Fuck man, why don't you throw somethin' at 'em?" said Zizi. "How about that empty coke bottle over there on the coffee table?"

That was all the prompting Cheetah needed. He opened the window and hurled the bottle out in the street. Although he was not actually aiming at the two men in blue, the bottle crashed at their feet with an explosion. The cops looked up to the third floor of the house and saw the open window. Word had gone out for some time, now, to keep an eye on 1090 Page Street, because of the Wednesday night jams and the longhairs that came and went, not to mention the smell of illegal substances.

They decided to call in to Park Station. A decision was made to send reinforcements and enter the house through the back door, which they did a little after two in the morning on Thursday. The residents heard the hullabaloo and scrambled to find out what was going on. The four policemen who broke into the house then began checking IDs and taking names. One resident, Vince Dalviso, was ordered to open his closet, where the cops found a small amount of grass. Dalviso was taken into custody and charged with the illegal possession of narcotics. "This is an illegal bust," protested the tenants. The cops laughed at those remarks and told them to take that up with their lawyers.

Early that morning handbills were circulating on Haight Street about the bust, for which Dalviso faced a maximum penalty of ten years in prison.

An impromptu demonstration was organized down Haight Street to Park Station, with the noisy marchers winding their way through the heavy traffic amidst chants of "Illegal Bust!" and "Blue Fascism!" When they went past the Drogstore Café (forced by the local authorities to change the name from the original Drugstore Café) at the corner of Haight and Masonic, the customers inside were aroused. Two of those customers–Allen Cohen of the *Oracle* and artist Michael Bowen, arrested during a bust at Millbrook in 1965–were stunned.

"People are so angry!" said Allen. "Look at all this energy going to waste. All this negative energy! What do you think Mike? Any ideas on how to transform this into something positive? A positive, productive force,"

"You're right," said Mike. "There must be a way to turn things around."

"The Beast is attempting to take control of the Haight-Ashbury," said Allen.

"That gives me an idea," said Mike. "On October 6, 1966, LSD will become illegal in California."

"That's right," said Allen. "We need to organize something on that day. Something positive."

"A Prophesy…."

"A Declaration…."

"A Prophesy of a Declaration of Independence," they said together, laughing with enthusiasm.

Over the next few days they drafted a "declaration" and organized their event in the Panhandle of Golden Gate Park.

Lysergic acid diethylamide, LSD, acid. That's what turns on the psychedelic counterculture and blows people's minds. The Haight couldn't have become the Haight without acid. It's called the Tibetan Third Eye because it navigates the pineal gland to alter consciousness.

On 6 October 1966, lysergic acid diethylamide became illegal in California. The love generation was quick to react and see something sinister in the ban on LSD, especially since the 666 was associated with the Book of Revelation, chapter 13, verse 16, which deals with the Antichrist, also known as the "beast." "And he provides that no one will be able to buy or to sell, except the one who has the mark, either the name of the beast or the number of his name. Here is wisdom. Let him who has understanding calculate the number of the beast, for it is the number of a man. That number is 666."

"Mike, what do you see as the primary problem in the Haight-Ashbury?" asked Allen.

"Well, it seems to me that getting at the truth of anything is a major problem, so I'd say *communication* is seriously flawed. By that I mean communication between City Hall and the people in the neighborhood."

"Right on. And demonstrations are not working. We need to try something less confrontational, 'cause in a confrontation with the heat, we're always going to lose," said Allen.

"A typical case of action and reaction," said Mike.

"It would be a mistake to protest the moratorium of LSD. Instead of protesting the law, it would be a lot more effective to show the hypocrisy of the new law, but without the confrontation that'll only create bad vibes. A celebration of innocence would be a positive form of demonstration. The police are expecting a conflict, so we'll organize a celebration of transcendental consciousness, the holiness of life and the infinite beauty of the universe; in short, the absolute beauty of being."

To promote the spirit of celebration, people were

encouraged to "bear the color gold, bring photos of saints and gurus and heroes of the underground . . . children . . . flowers . . . flutes . . . drums . . . feathers . . . bands . . . beads . . . banners, flags, incense, chimes, gongs, cymbals . . . symbols, costumes and JOY."

A request was sent to the Parks and Recreation Department and invitations mailed to the Mayor, John Shelley, and City Hall. Shelley didn't like the tone of the invitation, which spoke of "the paranoia and separation with which the State wishes to divide and silence the increasing revolutionary sense of Californians." "Pompous hippies," he must have thought to himself. The Mayor was also invited to address the rally, but, of course, he wouldn't be caught dead at a "hippie extravaganza." Shelley felt no affinity for a subculture that transgressed *his* values. He did, however, make sure Police Chief Thomas J. Cahill had undercover cops present to monitor the event, maybe even call in the feds, because Kesey and his crowd might show up.

It is probably no coincidence that the first issue of *The San Francisco Oracle* came out just a couple of weeks prior to The Love Pageant Rally. "A Prophesy of A Declaration of Independence" on the last page of the paper addressed the issues of outmoded social paradigms, being isolated from one's consciousness, creating "revolutionary communities," the equality of all things and, most importantly, individual rights: freedom to dispose of one's body as one wishes, freedom to express joy and freedom to expand one's consciousness.

A Prophesy of a Declaration of Independence
When in the flow of human events it becomes necessary for the people to cease to recognize the obsolete social patterns which have isolated man from his consciousness and to create with the youthful energies of the world revolutionary communities of harmonious relations to which the two-billion-year-old life process entitles them, a decent respect to the opinions of mankind should declare the causes which impel them to this creation. . . . We hold these experiences to be self-evident, that all is equal, that the creation endows us with certain inalienable rights, that among these are: the freedom of body, the pursuit of joy, and the expansion of consciousness . . . and that to secure these rights, we the citizens of the earth declare our love and compassion for all conflicting hate-carrying men and women of the world.

We declare the identity of flesh and consciousness. All reason and law must respect and protect this holy identity.

A large crowd attended the Rally presented as the "first public outdoor rock concert." The Grateful Dead, Big Brother and the Holding Company and the Joe Henderson Quartet played for free. All kinds of people grooved during the celebration. There were freaks, straights, children, parents, Hell's Angels, a variety of ethnic groups, and some of Kesey's crowd in and around his bus called Further. Narcotics agents were hoping to nab the runaway author, but he was nowhere to be found. Cahill's plainclothes officers were conspicuous with their notepads. Bobby Beausoleil–later associated with Charles Manson–was taking in the sights in a top hat.

French film celebrity Christian Marquand, who appeared alongside Brigitte Bardot in *Et Dieu ... créa la femme* (*And God Created Woman*) drove to the happening in a big black limousine. Michael McClure was with him. Marquand was looking for a starlet for his film *Candy*. They'd been smoking some good weed and feeling high. Suddenly Marquand froze in his tracks. "There she is! It's Candy, my next star." A bulge was noticeable in his pants, and he found it hard to maintain. "Hi, gorgeous!" he said with his thick French accent. "Want to be a star in the movies?"

The flower child didn't know who he was, but

sensed the exploitative vibes and told him to have sex with himself. Before he could say: *you bet your sweet bippy!* she'd vanished into thin air.

Richard Alpert, Timothy Leary's famous psilocybin associate at Harvard, was at the 666 celebration, too. Bowen called out to Alpert when he saw him and they said hello. "Say, Mike, how are things? Your Love Pageant Rally is really cool."

"Yeah," agreed Mike. "The vibes are really cool. Say, what would *you* call this event?"

"Well, now," thought Rich. "It's a lot more than just a rally. It's . . . how shall I say, it's humans being together. That's it. It's a Human Be-In."

"Yeah, I can dig it. Human beings at a Human Be-In. We've got to do it again, only a lot bigger the next time, with thousands of groovy people groovin' in the Park."

"I can dig it."

6

Hippie Values

I went out to San Francisco State College and saw a notice that caught my eye. A group of professors was interested in the "hippie phenomenon" and decided to conduct a study to find out what some of their values were. They were interviewing people from the Haight-Ashbury, so I got in touch with the group to see what it was all about. As far as I could tell, there were about twelve professors involved in the study, and what surprised me was that they were not all in the sociology department. They were from a fairly diverse range of disciplines, including the French Department. In fact, I learned that Marianne, my French teacher, was involved in the research. She was a friend and taught me a lot, and not just about mother tongues.

One of the group's goals was to avoid the clichés of the establishment, but at the same time, they knew they had to answer questions about sex, drugs and rock 'n' roll.

In light of what was happening in San Francisco with the dance concert scene at the Avalon Ballroom, Matrix, Fillmore Auditorium and Winterland, it was obvious that rock 'n' roll was embedded in the psychedelic counterculture and that any understanding of that culture involved a serious analysis of rock music; and with the emergence of the San Francisco sound, it took on an added dimension. It seemed clear, to the counterculture at least, that rock music was part of the cultural revolution taking place in the industrialized nations of the world. Millions of LPs and singles were being sold, so the financial impact was enormous, and many felt it was the most important genre to come about for decades, if not centuries.

Of course it was all about youth and it moved the younger generation in a way that no other form of music could. When hippies spoke about their music, it was obvious that it transcended aural stimuli.

The San Francisco sound evolved over the years. Many musicians of the local bands began their careers as folkies. Rock was an expression of the immediate present, and the medium of the genre was the message, as were the songs themselves. It expressed freedom to young people and a means of rebelling against the establishment. Not surprisingly, there were plenty of songs about revolution and social change, or about rebelling against traditional values. In a world where people *can't get no satisfaction*, rock allowed them to yell and scream, dance, twist 'n' shout to the music's driving rhythms and feel really good. The older generation seemed to be afraid of feeling good, because they were too uptight.

Rock's revolutionary aura was not exclusively political, although it has been argued by some, and rightfully so, that everything is, to some extent, political. Rock music has always been a powerful social force, and that's why songs have been censored, because those in power know music influences the way people think. Protest singers like Pete Seeger, Joan Baez, Barry McGuire, Phil Ochs or Bob Dylan, just to name a few, were helping to change the way people thought about society. Blowing people's minds can have a greater long-term impact than blowing things up.

It could be argued that rock stars are not revolutionaries, and never could be, since they are part of a commercial system devoted to making hits, selling records and making money. Jefferson Airplane, probably the favorite rock band in the Haight, made a cheesy commercial for White Levis, with the slogan: "We love you." Don't *you* want somebody to love? Of course you do, and so does almost every human being. We mustn't forget that the Airplane lived in a cherry mansion on Fulton Street, complete with four ostentatious Greek pillars. The managers of the bands sure knew that the music was all about making money, but there's probably no point in counting the number of rock bands and singers that got righteously screwed by their not-particularly-honest managers.

Lyrics, too, expressed the values of the counterculture: what was good and what was bad, what behavior was to be imitated and what behavior was meant to be put down.

"All you need is love" it was believed, and the songs that sold usually evoked themes that extended or explored the psychedelic trip. Of course the notion of *love* varies from one person to the next. Aristotle and Plato spoke of seven different kinds of love: *eros, philia, storge, agape, ludus, pragma* and *philautia*, so things are a little more complicated than one might expect. The psychedelic counterculture sought to experience unselfish love, or *agape*, towards their brothers and sisters, but they did not reject passionate sex either. *Love me two times girl*, said Jim Morrison, and "Light My Fire," the phenomenal hit by the Doors, was in many ways a demand by the flower children for their constitutional right to happiness in the form of sex, which the older generation repeatedly said was obscene and a taboo.

Peace was an important theme of the love generation, and even if the word was not always explicitly mentioned in the lyrics, it was often suggested or alluded to in many ways. The peace the hippies were referring to was not just absence of war and annihilation, as expressed by Barry McGuire's song "The Eve of Destruction." Peace was also about being safe and secure in one's possessions and one's home, explicitly guaranteed by the Fourth Amendment: "The right of the people to be secure in their persons, houses, papers, and effects, against unreasonable searches and seizures, shall not be violated, and no warrants shall issue, but upon probable cause, supported by oath or affirmation, and particularly describing the place to be searched, and the persons or things to be seized." Reality was quite different, however, as unwarranted searches had become commonplace in the Haight-Ashbury and across the nation. "For What It's Worth" by Buffalo Springfield evokes police violence and police intimidation, something the counterculture was all too familiar with.

The dance concerts in the mythical ballrooms became symbolic gatherings where the devotees congregated with the commitment of revivalists, which is to say that the venues were the source of a spiritual revival, though not in the sense that Billy Graham and the older generation understood them to be. In a very basic sense, it was all about freedom. Rock 'n' roll helped people to be *free*, or at least to feel free as long as the song lasted. It helped them to shrug off the inhibitions imposed by corporate culture.

The sociological study sponsored by San Francisco State found that sex was another value of the psychedelic counterculture, and young people were not at all abashed to speak freely about it, unlike their parents, for whom it was an unmentionable topic, something considered obscene, though their prejudice was largely prompted by ignorance.

"Carpe diem," said the freaks that were motivated by the pleasure principle, and not particularly interested in deferring sexual gratification. Of course there was a downside to this. The Free Clinic at 558 Clayton Street was often overcrowded with young people diagnosed with some form of venereal disease. It wasn't cool to force sex on others, but it wasn't too cool to abstain from sexual pleasure either. The contraceptive pill helped to change sexual mores in the counterculture, and those moral attitudes spread like wildfire. Sexual repression was seen as a real bummer by the freaks of the Haight and basically a way of forcing the establishment's paranoid trip on everyone. Waiting for marriage to have sex was as old-fashioned as codpieces

and knickerbockers.

Music was revolutionary in the Haight-Ashbury and so was sex. If feelings of guilt over sex were on the decline nationwide, it was because the counterculture was in the vanguard of the revolution. Accepting one's physical body and one's human desires as normal were part of higher consciousness. Psychological hang-ups related to sex kept one from achieving a higher and healthier sense of self. So many people in the older generation wanted their children to feel ashamed about making love, but the younger generation wasn't buying into that proposition. *P.O. Frisco – The San Francisco Oracle (The Renegade Oracle)* published an article entitled "The Craft of Masturbation," which sought to free people from guilt, although some who were working for the paper found the article rather cheesy. In a time of sexual liberation, the freaks of the Haight said that people were free to decide on the kinds of sex they wanted to practice.

Nudity was a significant element of sexual freedom and it was practiced by a fairly large number of hippies in the Haight-Ashbury. It was not uncommon to see groups of young people, both young men and young women, dancing nude on Hippie Hill in Golden Gate Park. Not all freaks were able to do that, of course, but the fact that some did is proof of its importance in the subculture.

It did not seem to be associated with voyeurism or exhibitionism, but more an adjunct or extension of sensuality and truthfulness. People in the Haight-Ashbury were seekers in the fullest sense of the word, and as such applied the Greek adage *Γνῶθι σεαυτόν (gnothi seauton),* know yourself. Men and women in the mainstream didn't know who they were and were not motivated to want to find out. Everyone played his or her prescribed role according to their profession and social status, acting within the narrowest of prescribed limits and stereotypes. It's not that people were shallow, they were hollow–there was really nothing inside. They were alienated from themselves. In a competitive world, other persons were perceived as threatening rivals, and spontaneity was not a part of their vacuous routine. After years of stultifying existence, their minds became closed to new ideas and sensations as they achieved vicarious thrills through television and the movies. The zombified creatures in subways, on trains or in cars, testify to the extent of the alienation.

Young people in the Haight-Ashbury did not want to become like the *living dead* of a system that eroded the very essence of humanity. They sought to explore the human experience, to learn, to grow and become whole, and nudity was one way of rejecting the trappings of a hollow existence. In many ways the counterculture was vilified because it dared to reveal the truth about the establishment and the negative consequences of adhering to its system.

The nudity of the counterculture had little if anything in common with the centerfolds of the girlie magazines that exemplified nudity as a commodity to be bought and sold, sexual fetishes that served the fantasies of frustrated men.

Unlike mainstream culture, which depicted nudity as a taboo and the human body as somehow obscene, the counterculture saw a healthy human body, particularly the female body, as beautiful and inspiring. This fact is made clear by the number of concert posters depicting naked or semi-naked women. The fact that nudity was generally prohibited, except perhaps in the smut sold in sex shops or on Broadway, meant that it could be used as a form of protest or implied protest. The fact that the nudity of very small children was tolerated by the establishment also meant that it symbolized innocence and the lack of corruption. Society, said the counterculture, was inherently corrupt, so by taking off one's clothes, one could symbolically achieve a form of innocence and be born again.

According to San Francisco State professors,

marijuana, hashish and psychedelic drugs were widely used by the counterculture in the Haight. They pointed out, too, that a distinction was made between *drugs* and *dope*. Basically, marijuana, hashish and psychedelics such as LSD and mescaline were seen as beneficial psychoactive substances, whereas speed, barbiturates, cocaine and heroin were viewed as harmful. Expanding one's consciousness was a goal of the counterculture, and things that could bring that about were believed to be positive. Some would later say that amphetamines brought about the demise of the Haight-Ashbury. Although used as stimulants to enhance alertness and performance, adverse side effects such as hypertension, stroke, depression, anxiety, aggressiveness and insomnia have been cited. Alcohol and nicotine, the primary drugs of the older generation, were viewed by the counterculture as negative substances. LEMAR International, the group that sought to legalize marijuana, generally agreed that the political and penal apparatus of the state imposed oppressive laws to prevent people from expanding their consciousness. Grass made them feel good, whereas liquor brought you down. It helped to expand a person's consciousness and see things in a new light, and dancing and listening to music were a lot more fun after smoking pot or dropping acid.

Smoking a joint could bring about profound insights about oneself, one's relationships with others, society, life, death and a wide range of topics.

The counterculture of the Haight-Ashbury was not using dope just for kicks, although that was the perception of the establishment. Hippies smoked dope to feel good and escape the banality of straight life, but they also smoked it as people seeking a more complete human existence.

Although young people in the counterculture were usually perceived as "drop outs" and "lazy," because they didn't like to work, that perception was fundamentally flawed. In truth, hippies were opposed to the unpleasant work from nine to five that their parents were forced to accept like slaves. People working on underground newspapers, writing poetry or fiction, interpreting horoscopes, playing rock music, drawing posters or organizing dance concerts, could spend an enormous amount of time doing it. The essential point is that they wanted their work to be rewarding and not stultifying. They knew that most people hated the work they had to do. The hippies in the Haight-Ashbury wanted their work to be interesting and, as much as possible, fun. This explains why many rejected the kinds of jobs that most people were forced to do. It is also true that there were not that many ways of supporting oneself in the neighborhood. One way of making enough to pay the rent and have something left over was to sell dope, but ripping someone off was a bummer.

In this sense, the hippies were not capitalists. They were not out to make a big profit and were opposed to the false values of consumer culture, typified by the majority of White Anglo-Saxon Protestants. Capitalism, argued the hippies, was based primarily on greed. The profit motive failed to take into account the essential needs of the people, while market competition favored large multinational corporations. The Diggers were adamantly opposed to it and were even against the small shops on Haight Street, most of which were struggling to survive. The Psychedelic Shop, for example, was several thousand dollars in debt. Moreover, the counterculture was not ignorant about the cutthroat practices of capitalists, and the fact that enormous waste and pollution were byproducts of the economic system. Some people in the Haight who were well-read in the Bible, liked to cite well-known biblical references, such as "The rich rules over the poor, and the borrower is the slave of the lender" (Proverbs 22:7); "No one can serve two masters, for either he will hate the one and love the other, or he will be devoted to the one and despise the other. You cannot serve God and money (Matthew 6:24); "He who loves money will not be satisfied with money, nor he who loves wealth with his income; this also is vanity" (Ecclesiastes 5:10).

Freedom was also recognized by those in the Behavioral Sciences as a key component of the Haight-Ashbury counterculture, at least from 1965 to early 1967. Hippies most definitely had principles, yet we all know that ideals can be perverted and destroyed. After the Human Be-In, the once peaceful neighborhood became progressively more violent and dangerous, as more and more adolescents poured into the Haight. Hippies wanted to create their own society in which people could do what they wanted to without being hassled by police or the establishment. They wanted to be free to smoke dope, use psychedelics, gather on the streets that they said belonged to the people, be exempt from military service, which they thought would be ended, do the kind of work they found gratifying, dance nude in Golden Gate Park (if they wanted to), organize rock concerts in the Panhandle, and so on. Many of these expressions of freedom were not possible because of laws or because of harassment by police and the local authorities.

7

Ken and Bill

Everybody in the Haight knew Bill Graham because he promoted dance concerts at Fillmore Auditorium and Winterland. Things really started humming for Bill when he organized benefit concerts for the San Francisco Mime Troupe that he managed. The first benefit took place in a tired old loft on Howard Street on November 6, 1965. *Holy schmoley, I've found Aladdin's lamp*, he thought as the sound of cash registers reverberated in his brain. He could plainly see what live music concerts meant to young people who were eagerly handing over money to dance and listen to music. It was easy to leave the Mime Troupe where he wasn't making a decent living; the spin off was organizing dance concerts at the Fillmore and Winterland.

Very few people knew that Bill's name at birth was Wulf Wolodia Grajonca. That's because he didn't like to remember the scenes from Nazi Germany. His mother rushed to get him out because of the increased oppression of Jews. Although Bill wouldn't talk about it, those events helped to shape his life and make him very competitive.

Most people know Ken Kesey for his inspirational novel *One Flew over the Cuckoo's Nest*, a bestseller that made Ken a celebrity overnight and provided him with the money he needed to bring his psychedelic fantasies to life. But he wrote only one other successful novel after that, preferring to goof off with a group of crazies known as the Merry Pranksters. For somebody who reportedly had so much trouble with grammar, it's amazing that he managed to write such a powerful work of fiction. Ken was not that great a public speaker either, since acid is not known for making people particularly articulate. The Acid Tests were his hallmark–people dropping strong doses of LSD and trying to keep it together. Some said he was more at ease with motorcycle gangs like the Hell's Angels. Ken Kesey shares at least some of Randle McMurphy's values. Ken and his fictional character reject conformity and authoritarianism; they love wild, uninhibited lives in which masculinity and physical strength are valued. Both were arrested by the police and sent to prison, too.

Ken and Bill were exact opposites. Bill Graham was straighter than straight, while Ken Kesey was taking double doses of LSD to make the trips as freaky as possible. Although he wrote *One Flew over the Cuckoo's Nest* on acid, the hallucinogen didn't help his creative impulse from there on out, at least as far as literature is concerned.

Ken and Bill's first encounter was at the Trips Festival. I was living on Waller Street at the time when an affable chick gave me a handbill for the event. I'm sure I didn't really understand what they were talking about, but the three day event from 21 to 23 January 1966, was tabbed as being an electronic experience. One eye-catching handbill announced the festival in bold letters with an optical art pattern in the center and the place and location on the bottom. The organizers–Zack Stewart, Stewart Brand, Ramon Sender and Ken Kesey–as it turned out, were absolutely right when they said it would be unusual, "the first gathering of its kind." That sure didn't deter spectators.

Bill, whose reputation as Mr. Money had grown in the Haight, was asked to help out, probably because things were not making any real headway.

Since Kesey was involved in the event, the Merry Pranksters were on the bus, too, so any and all high jinks were to be expected. Ken, who'd already been busted for grass, was arrested again the night before and was facing serious charges and several years behind bars. The publicity caused by his latest bust, plus the fact that he was released on bail in time for the festival, meant that a large crowd was assured. So Kesey was there, but he was disguised in a space suit with a helmet, so people outside his circle didn't know who it was.

Ken and the Pranksters were total acid heads, but since Bill was straight, that provided for a potentially explosive situation. Bill didn't like the idea of people using mind-bending drugs because they didn't always know what they were getting into. Later, of course, Bill's customers were mostly into acid and grass. The Trips Festival was essentially an elaborate Acid Test, and acid was available to everyone, including children, in the form of ice cream. How a child's mind could deal with the hallucinations is anybody's guess. For Ken, taking acid was a test to see who could handle its weirdness, and he liked to go to the extremes, probably because he liked the idea of provoking danger. Maybe that explains his association with the tough Hell's Angels. Timothy Leary, on the other hand, believed in set and setting; in other words a person needed to prepare their trip before blasting off into outer space.

With thousands of people stoned on acid, things got way out of control; and Bill, who up to that point knew nothing about the effects of LSD, was doing his best to control the uncontrollable, sort of like arranging the deck chairs on the Titanic. Plenty of people around Bill wanted to get him stoned, but couldn't figure out how to do it. Running around the crazy hall and clutching desperately onto his clipboard, you could see he was scared stiff by the acid trips. But he could also see that you could make a lot of money on psychedelic madness.

On Saturday the Merry Pranksters began setting up some scaffolding in the middle of the hall. Bill knew that everything had to be in the right place and that the scaffolding was all wrong. He approached the Pranksters to say he didn't like it, but they told him to see Ken about it. "So where's Ken?" asked Bill. "He's not here, yet," they said.

When the doors were about to be opened to let ticket holders inside, Hell's Angels came pouring into the hall from the back door like bats out of hell. Ken, in his space suit and helmet, was holding the door open for his friends. "What are you doing," asked Bill. "Why are these people coming in for free?" Kesey turned to look at the guy who was talking, and then calmly went back to what he was doing. Bill tried to shut the door on the gate-crashers, but couldn't because of the flow of crazies. Bill wanted an answer and started raising his voice: "What the fuck do you think you're doing?"

They were losing money because the Hell's Angels were coming in for *free!* And then it dawned on Bill that this must be Ken Kesey. The first encounter ended when Ken turned to Bill, flipped down his visor, and walked away. Bill got into a serious squabble with the Prankster Ken Babbs, too, but those guys were running the show that night, so there wasn't a hell of a lot he could do. From then on, Bill knew what to expect from Kesey and the Merry Pranksters.

Another time Kesey and the Pranksters wanted to organize an Acid Test at Winterland, at 1904 Post Street. Neal Cassady, depicted as Dean Moriarty in Jack Kerouac's *On the Road*, went to see Bill about renting the hall for an Acid Test Graduation. It was late Friday night and Bill didn't want to talk about it. Cassady was just as crazy as Kesey, maybe even crazier.

"It's late, Neal. We'll talk about it on Monday," said Bill.

"Oh, no man. We've got to do this thing now. Right *now* man."

Bill locked up the Fillmore as quick as he could to get out in the street. Neal made some reference to Bill's obsession about money and it cut to the quick; and then he went in even deeper by saying it was all about Bill's soul.

Bill was aware of Kesey's influence on young

people and the counterculture, but he was afraid Ken didn't know how to handle it. A rumor was circulating at the time, God knows what it was based on, that Owsley and Kesey were going to get everybody stoned out of their minds on acid by spiking the water supply, the food, the drinks, even the door handles at Winterland. Kesey was on some sort of a crusade to change the world with LSD. He'd gotten the Hell's Angels stoned, too, but it didn't seem to do much good. With drugs it's always a question of dosage, and sometimes the doses were *way* too strong at the Acid Tests. That only assured a lot of freak-outs.

Bill got in touch with Chet Helms, his rival promoter, to see if he knew what was going on. Chet called the right person who said Kesey was going to dose everybody, get them all stoned out of their gourds. When Bill heard that, he pulled the plug on the graduation ceremony.

Eventually, the Acid Tests came to a halt, and Kesey and the Merry Pranksters moved up to Oregon, where Ken had grown up.

Charlie

Charlie was a strange dude. He was in his early thirties and had apparently decided to let his hair grow long and to grow a moustache and a goatee. He was short and thin and his clothes were worn and dirty. A few people had gathered around him in the Panhandle where he was banging away on his guitar. He had some talent as a singer and musician as he sang loudly, sometimes almost yelling with frenzied exuberance, like a man possessed, or just angry at the world.

When he finished playing, I started a conversation with him and then we went to the Drogstore for a cup of coffee. I asked him about his music to get him talking, but he didn't need much coaxing because he was chatty, although his ideas were sometimes hard to follow. He told me his name and said he'd been sleeping in the park, in crash-pads and pretty much wherever he could. He fiddled constantly with his goatee as he spoke. I asked him where he was from and what he was doing.

I just got out of jail, man. In fact, I've spent half of my fuckin' life in jails. That's because people like me are not wanted, so they put us in cages 'cause we're not playing society's games.

I don't know this world anymore, man. Everything's goin' so fast, I can't keep up with it. It's like trying to catch up with a rocket on roller skates.

Everybody's talking about the Summer of Love, so I had to see for myself what it was all about. All these pretties running 'round with no panties or bras, asking for love, beggin' to get screwed. Man, this is paradise for me. But the Flower Power thing is on the decline, ya see. A lot of people have already lost their innocence and bartered their souls.

I told Charlie I was interested in his style of music and wondered where he got his material.

Music is my thing, man. You dig what I'm sayin'? For me, it's a form of communication. I write my own songs to let people know where I'm at. And the girls get turned on by the music, it attracts pussies like flies, and I'm a spider, he says laughing. I play wherever I can: in the park, on the street, in houses. . . . Sometimes I hitchhike across the Bay to Berkeley and play at the university. Students there dig my music and some put money in my can. But I'm not doing it for the bread, man, but because it makes me feel free and because it's a good way to make friends. I'm a musician by profession and someday I'll head south to get a recording contract in LA. Who knows, maybe I'll sign a contract with Universal or some other big company. I've got plenty of songs to make an album.

I was curious about his being in prison, so I asked him about it.

I'm an outlaw and a little kid 'cause I've been in the joint all my life. But prison is a state of mind, too. We all make our own prisons with the way we think. Charlie knows the score, you dig? I know how to survive in prison. I see all these crazies goin' helter skelter on the outside and I'm sayin' they're in prisons of their own. I can learn something from anybody, and I learned a lot from wardens, prison guards, parole officers and prisoners.

My thing is rebirth, man. I started the rebirth movement. Rebirth! Rebirth! he says loudly with wide eyes. You know what that is? You don't pick up the same shit. You start from scratch, all over again. And I live one day at a time, 'cause I'm in the here and now. Charlie knows the score. The waves go in and the waves out. That's the way it is.

Let me run somethin' to you. I don't like grown-ups. I like kids. Kids are honest, they tell you the truth. But adults are too busy playing mind games to tell the truth.

They don't even know what the truth is. They've forgotten what it is. And I'm mad. Oh boy I'm mad ya see. Our governors are all crooks. They're running our lives and they're ruining our lives. They're destroying the planet. The water is polluted, the air is polluted, they're cutting down all the trees, and what for? To make a lotta money. They're destroying our future, my future. They're destroying our children's future. But we're not gonna let 'em. God is not gonna let 'em do it. Life is God and God is life. And I'm the Pope, he says with his eyes bulging. I'm the Pope of love and hate, he says laughing. All these crazies are kneeling to their God on a cross. Bullshit, man. That's just one more death wish; and they've got plenty of those. I know and when you know you know, you know? We're gonna change the world. You dig what I'm sayin'? We're gonna change the fuckin' world. That's part of our rebirth movement. Jesus Christ is a reality, man. He died so I could live and so you could live. And believe me, I'm sure as hell not gonna miss out on somethin' like that. Hell no. If there was real justice in this world, we'd all be in trouble, wouldn't we? That's why we've got Jesus, man. He gets us out of a lot of shit that we can't deal with.

But a lot of people thrive on hate. They need hate to live, to justify their insanity. They use TV to poison our minds. People will believe whatever they see on TV. It poisons their fuckin' minds, man. That means that millions of people don't know who they are. So I ask them: Who is your reality? We're gonna start one big family and it will be a family of the soul. And I'll be the guru! he says with demonical laughter.

9

Astral Voyages

There were some people referred to as *mystics* giving a talk about astral voyages at the I/Thou coffee shop. I went there to see what it was all about. I knew that *astral voyage* was an esoteric word used to describe out-of-body experiences, and that some people said they used LSD to do it. Others claimed there was a slim cord attached to both bodies. Swedenborg had written about his personal astral voyages, but that was about all I knew on the subject. The guy giving the talk was called Sri something-or-other; he had an Indian name that I didn't fully understand because the group next to me was talking so much. There was a pretty large crowd present, including some fellas from the *Oracle*. A lot of the talk was a sort of how-to, or explanation on out-of-body experiences.

The following is a loose transcription of that talk.

Good evening, everyone. I'm going to say a few

things about astral voyages. Many people in the Haight-Ashbury are attempting to undertake these psychic trips, and I want to give you a few tips. Different peoples of the world have been going on astral voyages or journeys for thousands of years, so it's nothing new, I can assure you of that.

Astral voyages may be conscious or unconscious, but the conscious voyages, the kind that involve the will of the aspirant, are more important than the unconscious ones, which sometimes occur in our sleep.

It is important to remember that we are all spiritual beings. However, we are spiritual beings in a physical body in a physical world. Our physical body is limited— we cannot normally do things outside of our body. But our spirit is infinite and thus eternal. In this sense an astral voyage means traveling beyond our physical body. We all have a spiritual body, and so we all have the ability to undertake an astral voyage. We may have done it before as children without knowing what it was. Children might have an easier time doing it because they are less conditioned than adults.

But before doing this, there are some important things you need to know. One thing you should know about these journeys is that they involve a form of expanded consciousness. But what is consciousness? In a literal sense, consciousness is about being aware of our thoughts, sensations, feelings, the environment and everything around us. But the spirit is our higher consciousness. Everyone has it, but not everyone uses it the same way or to the same extent.

To discover this spirit we have to leave our physical body. Why? Because our material world is finite and the spiritual world is infinite. Our ego holds us back with fear, skepticism and other negative emotions that chain us to the material world we have become accustomed to. So it is easier to do if we are like children, eager to explore and eager to learn. Didn't the prophet say that those who enter the kingdom of the Lord must be like children?

Out-of-body experiences are extraordinary experiences, and they are way-out, to use one of the favorite expressions in the Haight-Ashbury. And because they are so unusual, some people, if not most, will be afraid. Your ego tells you that if you leave your body, you won't be able to get back. Fear often holds us back from doing things in life. But this fear is false. What usually happens when we are frightened by the voyage is that we immediately come back to our body, and the voyage ends abruptly. That's how it works.

To successfully travel in the astral plane you have to shut off fear, shut off the mind and vibrate with the Eternal. Remember that all existence is vibration, all is one, everything is interconnected, and if you can understand that truth, your voyages will be better. Now I see some of you smirking with skepticism and maybe wondering why I use the word voyage or journey but not trip. I do not live in your neighborhood, but I've listened enough to some of you to know that you call a trip a drug experience. An astral voyage is not a drug experience, and it is better not to use drugs to go on an astral voyage, because your spirit may not be in control of the journey; the drug will be in control. Childlike innocence and a non judgmental attitude are probably best for voyaging in the astral realm. We also need faith in ourselves, our true self. The ego mind, which wants to control what we do, tells us to be afraid because the ego cannot be in control on these voyages.

Voyaging through the astral plane may be a revelation for many, a sort of epiphany. But the ego does not like this perception and shuts it out; it builds a wall, like the boundaries formed by our different nations.

You all speak about love in the Haight-Ashbury, and love is useful during astral travel. Do astral travel with a feeling of love, not a feeling of selfishness. Love is light, and traveling in areas of light is better. But there are also areas of darkness, and I have spoken to some who have explored these regions. If there are angels on the astral plane, or messengers of light, there are also demons of darkness. You cannot have one without the other. The demons habitually frequent the regions of darkness, and they may try to seduce you, to pull you in, to distract you. So I would avoid the regions of darkness because these demons can pervert your thought and perception, so beware.

So where do you want to go? You can choose a destination here on earth or somewhere in outer space. If you concentrate on images of your destination, it will help you during your voyage. When you first begin, it is best to choose a specific destination. Before you undertake such a journey, you need to prepare yourself and the space around you. Meditate to achieve a feeling of peace and tranquility. Don't undertake these voyages if you feel uncomfortable and nervous. That will only result in a bad trip, if you will excuse the pun. Before you begin your out-of-body experience, you can also create a protective sphere around yourselves, a sacred space. This may be done in several ways: by chanting certain benevolent mantras and by creating energy spheres around your body with circular movements of your hands and arms.

In conclusion, let me say that existence is sacred. All life is sacred. Try to remember that in the astral plane. Open yourselves. Shut off your minds. Do not *fear. Have a purpose in mind and say to yourself that you will come back. The best journeys are those in which you prepare your return voyage.*

When the speaker finished his exposé, there was considerable excitement in the café. As he smiled at his audience, I thought I was looking at an immaterial vision, *at something that wasn't really there.*

10

Free Food

I'd never heard of the Diggers before I moved to the Haight, but despite their desire for anonymity, they seemed to have a real impact on the neighborhood. The more I asked people about the group, the more I realized they had sway in different aspects of the Haight-Ashbury, at least when it was still a community.

I saw a broadside pasted on a store window that said: FREE FOOD EVERYDAY FREE FOOD. IT'S FREE BECAUSE IT'S YOURS. The free food was distributed in the Panhandle at 4 p.m. every day.

A few days later I was walking down Oak Street and saw about twenty-five or thirty people gathered in the Panhandle. It must have been about a quarter to four. I walked towards the group to see what was going on.

There was a large wooden frame painted orange. It must have been at least twelve feet by twelve feet. The people were pretty young. Some of them were in their early twenties and even younger. Most of them were guys. I only saw a couple of girls. Some were sitting and some were standing. I noticed that most of them were holding bowls. The people I spoke to said they came on a fairly regular basis, although they tried to avoid weekends because there were too many people on those days. They lived in the Haight for the most part, but a few came from other neighborhoods. They were definitely *not* from the affluent classes.

After a while a truck pulled up and some guys got out and unloaded a milk can and some other stuff. The crowd recognized them immediately and seemed somehow to express silent relief. I asked what was being served and they said stew, bread and maybe some fruit. The menu varied from one day to the next depending on what the Diggers could scrounge or steal.

I was told that most of the food was acquired for free. A lot of it had been thrown away because it couldn't be sold. The day old bread came from bakeries, the vegetables came from supermarkets, and the poultry and meat were things that most people didn't want to eat, like chicken necks or pigs' feet.

To be served you had to walk through the large orange frame–the free food was waiting on the other side. As some people walked through the frame, apparently a purely symbolic gesture, I heard someone say they were passing through a "free frame of reference" and thereby changing their perception of reality. After all, when you do something for free, you do it in *a free frame of reference.*

I didn't have a bowl, so I settled for a slice or two of day old bread, just to get involved. When I asked the guys who brought the stuff why they did it, they said it was their way of taking responsibility by helping people out. When people went through the frame, they were also taking responsibility by changing their attitudes and the way they lived, by realizing the true meanings of words like *money* and *free.* Diggers, they said, chose to act to solve social problems, rather than by just saying what needed to be done. They called that *creating the condition you describe.* They used catchy phrases to represent their ideas, such as *do your own thing* and *we live our protest.* From that I gathered that they were revolutionaries of a sort, though their means of changing society were different. We agreed that money corrupts human relationships by putting the emphasis on the money. People didn't help one another because it was the right thing to do, but because they could get money out of it.

The Diggers were outspoken about what they were doing and when I asked them what they thought about the neighborhood, they were quick to respond. The hippies were "apathetic," they said. A lot of them just wanted to get stoned and have a good time, but that attitude would not change the political environment of the military-industrial complex. They were also quick to attack the merchants on Haight-Street, whom they said were basically playing the same games as mainstream society, though to a lesser degree. The rock bands, too, they pointed out, were hypocrites, dressed up as hippies to attract followers who would buy their records and pay money to see them play at the dance concerts. All their songs about love, freedom and getting together were a lot of baloney.

Did the Diggers expect to eliminate poverty? Certainly not, at least that's what they told me. With free food, crash pads, a free store and guerilla theatre on Haight Street, they did, however, hope to change attitudes and behavior, and put people in a free frame of reference.

What about the name Diggers, why did they choose that? They said they borrowed the name from the seventeenth century Diggers in England, who opposed the monarchy and the capitalist system. The English Diggers urged their countrymen to seize the land that had been taken away from them and to work in egalitarian communities. They sought to create a classless society. Of course they were fighting the most powerful government in the world. The idea that money corrupts and that goods should be acquired without money was expressed in their pamphlet entitled *A Declaration from the Poor Oppressed People of England.* Many of their ideas are also expressed in the Bible: "Come, all you who are thirsty, come to the waters; and you who have no money, come, buy and eat! Come, buy wine and milk without money and without cost" (Isaiah 55:1).

I thanked the Diggers for the information and their generosity. Their response: "Just remember to do your own thing . . . *for free.*"

11

The Prophet

A spiritual get-together was scheduled at Mount Tamalpais, the sacred Miwok Mountain, on the weekend. Posters in the hippie boutiques simply announced the happening as "The Prophet Speaks." Rumor had it that people at the *Oracle* and the Psychedelic Shop had organized the event. Everyone was cordially invited. There was no fee, but donations would be accepted. I figured I didn't have anything to lose and was intrigued by the title.

When I got to the historic mountain there were people chanting things I didn't understand and the air was perfumed with different fragrances.

There was already a large crowd, but I managed to find a place to sit not too far from the improvised stage. I sat down and waited for things to begin. Candles were lit, incense was burning and two musicians were playing traditional Lebanese music. One man was playing an oud and the other a derbake, or Arabian drum. Their music seemed to create a mysterious feeling of enchantment and wonder. Other robed persons were moving about discreetly, apparently in preparation of the presentation.

After a while the music stopped and a man in a white robe appeared. People around me were whispering, "Oh, it's the prophet!" He approached the microphone and said he was pleased to be there to speak about certain universal truths he had discovered during his religious pilgrimages and meditations. He seemed to be surrounded by an aureole of aureate light, or was I just too stoned?

"What is it you wish to know?" he asked.

Someone in the audience spoke up immediately, "Speak to us about good and evil."

"We wish to do good, but sometimes end up by doing bad things to ourselves and others," he began. "Is it because we have forgotten the difference between the two, or is it because we have forgotten who we are? The Greek philosophers said we must know who we are. When we know who we are and are always conscious of that knowledge, it will be more difficult for us to harm others or say hateful things. But we forget who we *really* are. When we know who we are, we are generous and caring. When we do not know, we can be selfish and hateful. If we see Eternity in a drop of water, we will usually strive to do good deeds. But it is also a question of *knowing*, not merely of *believing*. We can believe anything we wish. We can believe that the earth is flat if we want to, or that the moon is made of Swiss cheese (laughter in the audience).

"Few are those who have attained this knowledge in our world. And why is that? Because we do not have the time to know such things, and we have little interest in discovering them, or meditating on serious questions. When you look around you, what do you see? What do you feel? Can you see that the universe is in a state of continuous vibration and that we are vibrating with it, that we are part of it and that it is part of us?

"Please, do not misunderstand my words. What I am describing is not a drug-induced vision, although some who have ingested psychedelic substances may have had such visions.

"Do you understand what I am saying? The world is one. All the separations society has created are merely illusions to fool us. They are not real, though they are reinforced every day in our minds by society.

"To do good we must be conscious, fully conscious of what we do and say. We must achieve a higher state of consciousness to understand who we are and what our relationship to the world really is. When we comprehend this, we will find it difficult to do evil, because we will realize we are hurting ourselves. This is sometimes called *moksha* or *vimukti*, which means enlightenment. The Japanese call this experience *satori*, which means understanding and seeing one's true nature.

At this point, the speaker made a sign to the musicians who punctuated his remarks with a brief melody.

When they had concluded, someone in the audience said, "Speak to us about the problems of sex." This request brought muffled laughter from some parts of the crowd.

"I will speak to you of sex because we are all concerned, are we not? Not just the hippies in the Haight-Ashbury with their Love-Ins.

"But why is it a problem for us? Is the sexual act itself the problem, or is it something else, like our fantasies, our obsessions, our role playing and our projections of a natural act in nature? Assuredly, it is not the act itself that is a problem for us, anymore than sitting down to a meal is a problem. No, the sexual act is not the problem, it is thinking about it, or more specifically, what we think *about* it that engenders problems. And we are encouraged by the media to think about it. As a result, we become obsessed with it. For some of you, it might be a game, a way of scoring points to prove your masculinity. Oh, I'm familiar with a few of your colloquialisms. You talk about *doing it, getting laid, screwing* and *scoring*. And you've invented some pretty vulgar expressions to describe the act itself, which says enough about the ways some human beings perceive it. It is the one great thing in life that helps people to forget how lost they are and how impoverished their lives are. But if you think about it, for a lot of people it is simply a way of glorifying their ego. Men boasting about their latest conquests has become a cliché that your movies reinforce to make you feel secure. For some women it is not the man that is important, but his position in life, the amount of money he makes, the car he drives, the clothes he wears or the way he combs his hair. Those examples are proof enough that the ego is involved. It is all about taking, not about sharing, giving pleasure to your partner, caring about your partner; no, it is about what *you* get out of the deal, what your ego gets out of it. When the ego gets involved and we project all our fantasies and obsessions onto it, it is going to become a problem, and the great liberating experience turns us into slaves. But we don't want to be slaves, do we? We want to be free.

"My generation, the older generation, has created all kinds of problems associated with sex, and older people are going to do their best to make sure that the younger generation–and I see that most of you are young–gets poisoned with the older generation's hang ups. Sexual perversions are all part of the ego's involvement in the sexual act. Maybe you need mirrors to get it off, or maybe you need to get dressed up in black leather, or maybe you need to be whipped or spanked. (laughter) The ego has a lot of imagination as far as that is concerned. No, as long as the ego is involved, there will be problems.

"And you cannot run away from the ego because you will take it with you wherever you go. Your problems will only cease when the ego has ceased to exist. So sex is not the problem, the problem is in your head, in your thoughts, in your ego. You need to understand the way your mind works. Follow your thoughts and see the way they glorify your ego.

"Sex has its place, but when it dominates our thoughts and our acts, when it becomes an obsession and when we project so many ideas onto it, naturally it will become a source of conflict that can disrupt our lives and make us unhappy. Our selfishness, our false ideals, our egos prevent us from expressing true love. And the next time you're invited to a Love-In, remember that."

At that moment, the musicians began another melody. People stood up with a general feeling of satisfaction, it seemed, and began to wander away, as though lost in thought. I thumbed my way back home with so many ideas ringing in my head, like the bells of a church on Christmas.

12

Now!

Spontaneity was a key attribute of the counterculture in the Haight-Ashbury. Young people living there had a lot of imagination, and expecting the unexpected was to be expected. After the Diggers were found not guilty for blocking traffic on Haight Street and immortalized by the *San Francisco Chronicle* on 30 November 1966, Hashbury's living legends eagerly sought new ways of celebrating spontaneity.

NOW! One simple word underscored the significance of guerilla theater whose existential events would probably have been valued for their exuberance by the likes of Albert Camus, Dino Buzzati or Simone de Beauvoir. The Mime Troupe's Home Guard was present, and the cavalry–Hell's Angels on thunder machines–was roaring up and down the asphalt. The counterculture didn't need any encouragement to cross swords, and com/co broadsides and word-of-mouth were enough to mobilize three to four thousand screaming troopers.

Bring audiences to liberated territory and thus create life-actors. That was part of the goal that implied reclaiming the territory of Haight Street, which City Hall mistakenly believed belonged to them. To heighten the madness, car mirrors, penny whistles, candles, incense sticks, lilies and posters printed with the word NOW in large red letters on white paper were distributed to the shock troops.

Soon the juggernaut had moved into action. Two columns stormed down Haight Street, chanting and yelling, first one group and then the next: "Oooooo!" "Ahhhhh!" "Shhhhhhhh!" "NOOOOW!" A strange echo effect was created by the ranks. In the midst of the mayhem, assailants would jam up the intersection, while flowers were lovingly handed out to passers-by. The reclaiming of territory brought traffic to a screeching halt. A few of the people in their cars joined in the battle, as did a municipal bus driver. The cavalry made itself conspicuous by roaring down the middle of the street. One girl, standing up on a Harley, howled the battle cry: "FREEEEEE!" Liberation at last! The boisterous battalion had reclaimed Haight Street.

Alas, such an extemporaneous show of freedom could not last forever, and police put an end to the victory celebration. For it was an illegal gathering; no one had applied for a permit, because it would have been denied anyway. What else could the militants do but sing out: "The streets belong to the people! The streets belong to the people!"

The police were itching to bust somebody, anybody, so they targeted Hairy Henry and Phyllis Wilner, the guy and the girl leading the assault down Haight Street. It was all in fun, but that was beside the point. The cops took his driver's license and called in to headquarters to see if he was wanted for anything. Bingo! They hit the jackpot because Henry had just recently gotten out of San Quentin prison and was on parole.

"Come along with us to the station, and you'll get your license there," said one of the cops.

"Shit, you know, you can just keep that damn license. I don't need it, anyway," said Henry.

Other cops who were watching came over to get in on the action.

"Well now we're taking you in for resisting arrest," said a cop.

"Resisting arrest? What arrest? Nobody said nothin' 'bout no arrest. I didn't do nothin' and ain't goin' nowhere," said Henry defiantly.

Another biker by the name of Chocolate George, who was popular in the Haight-Ashbury, plunged into the army of police to rescue his buddy, and a tug of war ensued, with the police trying to pull Henry into the paddy wagon and Chocolate George trying to pull him out. Predictably both bikers ended up by getting busted when the tug of war turned into a rugby match.

Diggers quickly reacted by yelling to the crowd and an impromptu demonstration began, with the marchers heading for Park Station. "Free Hairy Henry! Free Chocolate George!" they shouted, and a few other things that were less polite. A few crazies actually got inside the police station, but they were forced out at gunpoint. When the amount of bail to release the prisoners was made known, the crowd generously pitched in and the money was raised. The bikers were dumbfounded to see people they didn't know defending them.

Chocolate George had a happy ending; he was bailed out that night. Hairy Henry, on the other hand, was kept in jail pending the outcome of his trial for a minor traffic violation. The Diggers found a lawyer for Henry who agreed to defend his client for free.

Street events in the Haight-Ashbury, especially on Haight Street, often seemed to be confrontational. Many so-called hippies were opposed to traffic on Haight Street and believed that the streets really did belong to the people. But their complaints fell on deaf ears.

The Hell's Angels were well-established in the neighborhood, though most were living elsewhere, and often participated in events. They were adept at ignoring rules and flouting authority, an attitude which often resulted in a perpetual testing of limits. When gathered in groups their behavior could be nothing if not unpredictable

Peter Berg's idea of guerilla theater is largely confrontational, though more in a positive sense, since he wanted individuals to look within themselves to understand their motivations and social conditioning. Inevitably that resulted in conflicts with the *status quo* and the establishment, a necessary ingredient for social change. Those who are interested in theater know that it usually involves some form of confrontation, be it psychological, philosophical, social, political, economic or other.

It occurred to me that the street events in the Haight-Ashbury raised many questions about the meaning of democracy and civil liberty. Many of those issues would remain unanswered.

13

Madness at Glide Memorial Church

What's an invisible circus? I didn't have the foggiest notion. My suppositions were primarily based on a small handbill about the size of a postcard that I found at the Drogstore Café. An archaic circus wagon is represented with THE INVISIBLE CIRCUS in capital letters above it. A blue dove is flanked by two spotted monsters, and a blue and red tiger is poised to attack. The event was described as a seventy-two hour environmental community happening, whatever that was supposed to mean. The Glide Church Foundation, the Diggers and the Artists Liberation Front sponsored the happening.

Glide Memorial Church is an imposing edifice. It is not located in the Haight-Ashbury but at 330 Ellis Street in the Tenderloin district of San Francisco, a neighborhood associated with a variety of social problems including alcoholism and prostitution. The Glide Foundation was created by Lizzie Glide, wife of wealthy cattle rancher H. L. Glide. Lizzie bought the land in 1929 and construction began immediately.

The church had a history of collaborating on projects with artists and countercultural groups; that's why it was chosen by the organizers of The Invisible Circus. The word "circus" evokes different things for different people, but knowing that the Diggers were involved, I guessed that part of the motivation was to taunt the establishment and mainstream values, some of which were religious and spiritual. At least one thing seemed to be clear–the psychedelic counterculture of the Haight-Ashbury was being catered to. I remember being reminded to take a sleeping bag, because people were planning on crashing inside the building.

When you entered the church from the street, you had to take an elevator to the basement where you waded your way through piles of shredded plastic. The people I saw had trouble getting through the basement as they lost their balance and stumbled. No one got hurt, but it was difficult going, and my guess was that a lot of people were stoned.

The next obstacle to overcome was a recreation room with a very low ceiling. It was suffocating there because it was next to the boiler room. Rock music was played so loud that it made your ears throb, and groups of people grabbed at your most sensitive parts from everywhere. There was nothing to do but get out of the room as fast as you could.

The church cafeteria served as a place to relax. An oversized punch bowl on one of the tables was filled with a fruit drink that had been laced with LSD. There was no way of knowing how much one would take by drinking it. Some people, I noticed, drank from it twice.

Upstairs is where things got more serious. Different rooms were designated for different happenings. Some were for having sex, others for being quiet, others were forbidden, and so on. A riot of noise was coming from the sanctuary where people played flutes, drums, bells and the church's pipe organ. I chose a room where Lenore Kandel was reading people's feet. I took off my shoes and socks, and stretched out my legs. She began feeling my feet and toes and looking at the different lines. She assured me that feet never lie, that I should follow my feet wherever they took me, and that it was important to always put one's best foot forward.

Quite a few of the church offices were reserved for making love. Mattresses were covered with Indian bedspreads; candles and incense were lit and there were different perfumes and oils. Most of them were pretty busy.

One room was called "The John Dillinger Computer Service." Richard Brautigan, whom I'd seen in the

Panhandle, and Chester Anderson and Claude Hayward of the Communication Company, were busily printing news briefs to let people know what was going on in different parts of the church. They also gave people directions on how to get to the various happenings. Hundreds of flash bulletins were printed using their mimeograph machine. To get the news that was newsworthy, reporters went around the church to find out what was happening and then got back to the Computer Service where the news was printed and then circulated throughout the building.

A round table discussion "On the Meaning of Obscenity" took place at about nine o'clock p.m. Members of the panel included Peter Berg, a minister, a policeman in charge of public relations and a lawyer. The sometimes heated discussion was brought to a climax when a nude couple was carried ceremoniously into the room on a mattress by several strong men. They lowered the couple who began making love in front of the audience. At that moment, a group of belly dancers burst through a large sheet of paper and began dancing ecstatically around the copulating couple. The Glide Memorial officials, who had misgivings about the event in the beginning, would be stunned when they saw how far out of control things would get.

Alcoholics, bums, drag queens and prostitutes from

the Tenderloin attended the happening, as did a few Hell's Angels. Nothing was sacred in the church with the anything-goes-attitude of the participants, most of whom were totally wiped out on LSD. I suppose it was because they didn't know how big of a dose they'd taken. I was glad I hadn't touched the punch bowl.

People were exorcising their latent sexual fantasies at full tilt as they desecrated the historic place of worship. Some were running naked up and down the aisle, others were participating in group sex, hookers brought their clients from the street into the church, and one person was engaged in an act of cunnilingus on the altar, while others were performing ritualistic flagellations or fellatio. For many people LSD dissolves inhibitions.

I noticed a few cameramen and photographers from the local news media, but I couldn't see anyone talking to them. Not one word about The Invisible Circus was printed the next day in the papers, maybe because no one would have believed that things like that had actually happened in a San Francisco church, or maybe because church officials didn't want that kind of publicity.

Early in the morning police arrived at the church with fire marshals who presented court orders to vacate the premises. The John Dillinger Computer Service told everyone over the public address system to pick up their things and leave as soon as possible. They also mimeographed bulletins to the same effect.

Church officials were relieved that the whole thing was over. They must have realized that not much would be left of the church after three days of lunacy.

Thousands of people had attended The Invisible Circus and many more would have showed up if things had continued the way they did.

Pigpen (Ronald McKernan), the blues singer for the Grateful Dead, was supposed to play the church organ for Sunday's service, but that was cancelled, too, as a result of the mayhem that had gone on for hours.

The only way I could get back to my room on Waller Street was to walk. I'm a fast walker, so I didn't mind, and anyway, I didn't have much choice.

A couple of days later, com/co printed a flyer listing the church's grievances, the main ones anyhow. They felt there were way too many people in the church. It's impossible to say how many attended the happening, but there must have been several thousand. The church officials also objected to the pornographic films, the nudity and the lack of respect for church property, particularly the red carpet in the sanctuary that was ruined by burns and candle wax. Probably out of a sense of decency, the church officials didn't mention the orgies that had been going on.

In the aftermath of these events I asked myself a lot of questions. I recognized the importance of not forcing the dosage of psychedelics. Ken Kesey, or so it was said, was in the habit of taking large doses of acid. Maybe he could deal with it, but not everyone could. Some people freaked out and had a bad trip, which to me didn't seem to be a laughing matter. If you were dumping acid into a punch bowl, the way they did for The Invisible Circus and the Acid Tests, there was no way of knowing how much LSD you had taken.

The Invisible Circus was conceived as a liberating event, but was it? For some Diggers it was a reaction to the Human Be-In. Most people I know were fairly satisfied with the Be-In, but some Diggers sneered at it. As far as consciousness goes, many people at the Be-In raised their consciousness, but that didn't seem to be the case at The Invisible Circus, where there seemed to be a total disregard for the place they were in. The idea of *outré* was prevalent in the psychedelic counterculture, which often sought to test the limits of human experience. Rejecting mainstream values is one thing, but being excessive simply for the sake of excessiveness does not seem to guarantee a state of higher consciousness. Likewise, mayhem for the sake of mayhem will not create inner harmony or peace.

More than anything else, I saw The Invisible Circus as a theatrical event, a form of guerilla theater for which the Diggers were so fond.

People in the Haight-Ashbury often spoke about liberation and being free, but liberation can also be paradoxical. It is possible to become intrinsically bound to the thing one is trying to liberate oneself from. Liberation can also be played as a sort of game, the goal of which may be ego satisfaction and conflict rather than true liberation.

Meanwhile, back in the City, drugs were big news in the media, as the number of drug arrests was on the rise, clogging up the judicial system in Northern California. It was reported that lab technicians were unable to keep up with the number of substances they had to analyze.

A rock band from Denver, Colorado, by the name The Rainy Daze, *double entendre oblige*, released an album entitled *That Acapulco Gold*, and the single with the same name sold well on the charts. Of course everybody in the Haight-Ashbury knew that the song was about a particular strain of grass known for its golden color, pleasing taste and THC potency. The straights didn't know what it was about, but when the White House found out, they were irate, and the song, like so many other hits, was pulled from the radio because it promoted an illegal substance.

There were drug tragedies, too, unfortunately. On Sunday the twenty-sixth of February, a nineteen-year-old girl plunged to her death in the Haight-Ashbury when she fell, or maybe jumped, out of a window on the third floor. She was reportedly naked.

14

Selling the Oracle

The San Francisco Oracle was undoubtedly one of the most unusual underground newspapers ever published anywhere in the world, a mind blower and a cosmic voyage for its readers. Allen Cohen brought it to life after he had a vivid dream about a rainbow paper. It took a few editions for the colors to appear, but Cohen and the staff eventually printed the kind of paper they'd dreamed about. The first issue sold for fifteen cents, later for twenty-five cents and thirty-five cents out of state.

It was not strange to see hippies on street corners hawking the paper in the Haight. Some looked pretty ordinary, while others might be wearing leopard pants, sandals and all the hippie paraphernalia you could imagine.

I decided to sell a few copies one day, to join the tribe, so to speak, and went to 1371 Haight Street, the paper's headquarters, to check it out. I wasn't sure how many to take, but I asked for forty copies to start with. The mellow dudes at the *Oracle* intimated that that might be a lot to start with, but I was eager to try. I couldn't carry them all so I put most of them in a back pack and headed out on Haight Street with my artless sense of optimism. I'd been standing in the street for a while, but wasn't selling too many papers; I only sold two copies after more than an hour. One copy was for a group of teenagers in a car from the suburbs, and another was sold to someone on a bus riding through the neighborhood. They opened their window and asked for a copy. I had to hurry because the bus was pulling away and I wanted to get my twenty-five cents.

Next I tried a few of the shops on the street. I sold a copy at the Drogstore Café, but most of the other shops already had a copy. A barefoot hippie girl who looked like she'd been sleeping in the park stopped to chat and asked me how it was going. I said that not too many people were interested on Haight Street. She said that people she knew often borrowed a copy from someone else because they didn't have a lot of money. She suggested I try the Grateful Dead House at 710 Ashbury Street, the Airplane Mansion at 2400 Fulton Street, the Dog House at 2125 (home of the Family Dog concert production company, and Janis Joplin's apartment at 892 Noe Street. I figured what to hell.

Before she left, she asked if I had any spare change. I gave her the seventy-five cents I'd made by selling three copies, which made me feel good because it got a big smile from her.

710 Ashbury, home of the Dead, seemed like a good place to start. I knocked on the door and waited for a few seconds before a young, brown-haired girl dressed casually with a striped sweater came to open the door. You could smell marijuana when she did. I said I was selling the *Oracle* and asked if I could come in. She looked at me questioningly and then stepped aside so I could get by and invited me to have a seat in an armchair. Somebody was practicing guitar in one of the bedrooms, going over the same riffs several times to get it right. I noticed the plaster was falling from the ceiling. There were empty beer cans and dirty socks on the floor, large posters of Albert Einstein and W. C. Fields on the wall, and an American flag on the fireplace. When the girl came back I told her that my name was Louis-Bertrand, but that she could just call me Lou. She said her name was Mountain Girl, and then she disappeared for a while. When she reappeared other people started coming into the room. One skinny guy with long hair sat down with a plate and some grass and started rolling joints. Everyone in the house blew my mind by being so open and friendly. I asked them if

they read the *Oracle* and some said "yes," adding that they knew Allen Cohen, the Thelin brothers and pretty much everyone on the staff. I put a copy of the paper on a table and said it was on me. Then the joints were passed around. It was pretty good weed and before long everyone was laughing and joking. The musicians were talking about their next gig and about an Acid Test, and some were griping about Owsley's crazy diet of meat and milk, saying they were fed up. "Shit, we sneak out to delicatessens every chance we get. Mmmmm! How about some hot pastrami en rye, with French mustard and dill pickles?" said one guy.

"Ohhhh yeah! Sounds good! With some luscious potato salad and strawberry wine," said another.

"Say, you suckers are making my mouth water. Now don't forget the lox and bagels with cream cheese," said someone else.

"Ohhhhh! I'm for that, but don't forget the strawberry cheese cake for dessert," said another guy.

I asked them what the name of the band meant and how they chose it. A guy with long hair and glasses said that Jerry, their lead guitar, found the expression by leafing through a *Britannica World Language Dictionary*. The definition refers to the soul of a deceased person, or his angel, that shows gratitude to someone who arranges their burial. That sounded really groovy to the band members, so they kept it. "And who's the leader of your band?" I queried. They all pointed in different directions, some pointed to Jerry, also known as Captain Trips, but no one admitted to being the leader. "We don't really have a leader," said Jerry. "We're not the Beatles, you see. Actually, the *audience* is the leader. Some bands play *at* the audience, but we play *with* them. We pick up their vibes and see where it goes. It works for us, but it probably wouldn't work for other bands."

I looked around the house and said their pad was out of sight.

"Ah, it's a place to crash," said Pipgen, taking a swig from his Burgundy wine.

"We were in Paradise at Rancho Olompali," said Jerry. We had this huge Spanish style house, a swimming pool and a lot of land to do whatever we wanted to."

"Right on," said a guy with a tie-dyed T-shirt. "And all those bands hanging out to jam: Jefferson Airplane, Big Brother, Quicksilver, the Charlatans. . . . People totally fucked up on LSD, going bananas, jumping into the pool. Rock 'n' roll came to the Promised Land."

"So many good vibes in Novato," said Jerry with nostalgia.

I was interested to know something about their

musical style and what influenced it, so I asked if any music helped to form their particular sound.

Two members of the Dead spoke at the same time: "'Cleo's Back' by the soul band Junior Walker and the All Stars."

"'Cleo's Back' had a strong influence on our band," said Captain Trips. "We looked at that motherfucker inside and out. It reflected our particular style of playing. The instruments broke into the song in a kind of anything goes attitude; and there are so many little niches where musicians come in with good sounds. We call it the *conversational approach*. That's the way it works for us."

"We're into improvisation," added the guy in the tie-dyed T-shirt. "We're not necessarily into really tight structure, so we have to listen to each other when we jam. We go on a trip when we play and aren't sure where it's goin' to end. Sometimes Jerry will take off in a whole new direction, so we have to pick up on it to follow. Jazz is like that, more than rock music."

The conversation came around to LSD and a guy with long sideburns and long dark hair told me to be careful. "Acid is a two-sided coin, man. It'll blow your mind and then leave you stranded on a cliff . . . alone. It'll show you the truth about people, too.

"So where are you guys playing next," I asked. They

said different places at different times, so I wasn't really sure. Some guy said they might play on Haight Street, or in the Panhandle. "We get up in the morning and then figure out what we're gonna do. If we wanna play on Haight Street, we just call Sweet William and the right people and do it. We never ask for permission because the mayor doesn't like us."

I didn't want to overdo my welcome and I could sense they had some stuff to do, so I thanked them for the smoke and said I was going to try and sell some papers. One guy suggested I go to San Francisco State because the teachers and students were pretty cool out there.

Janis was not at home and neither was Jefferson Airplane, so I got on the tramway and headed for San Francisco State. But halfway there I realized that my initial enthusiasm was petering out, so I got off the tram and hitchhiked back to my place.

15

A Hopi Prophecy

Hopi myth and spiritual tradition are complex and interesting to study. The Hopi Indians have lived in the Southwest region of the United States since about 500 CE and probably came to North America thousands of years ago. I had read about the sacred snake dance, so when I heard that a Hopi Elder was going to talk about Hopi Prophecy at San Francisco State, I was eager to see what he had to say. The talk was being given in a class on Native American studies. The Elder would discuss the Hopi's Prophesy Rock and the path that mankind must take. When he was introduced, the audience applauded politely and then he began to speak.

On a sacred boulder is a diagram which the Hopis call Prophecy, and the boulder is referred to as Prophecy Rock. The story it tells is the emergence of the Hopi from the Third World. They had gone through three different worlds and the world we are in today is the Fourth World. Today, we have come to the edge of the Fourth World because of the society in which we live. Peoples of the world have accepted materialism, which rules most aspects of their lives. Thus our path is a materialistic path. But this path is all about the domination of science and technology. Our world is in trouble because it does not have a human heart. We are abandoning, or have already abandoned, the spiritual path, which is the path of our sacred ancestor who came from the Third World to the Fourth World. The name of this ancestor who lived off the land is Maasaw. He is an important figure because he is the protector of the land, the preserver of Mother Earth. If you look carefully at Prophecy Rock, you'll see that the material path ends abruptly, but the spiritual path does not end, it continues.

There is a picture of Maasaw at the start of the Fourth World. And he is also at the end of the Fourth World. This is important because it means that he is the first and the last, the alpha and the omega. He is holding onto an ear of corn, which is meant to give us confidence and show us that there is hope.

When you look at Maasaw's path, you see three circles, two of which are complete. The third circle is only half complete. These circles represent World War One, World War Two, and the war that is going on now. This means that Maasaw's path is being destroyed by war and pollution, for which mankind alone is responsible.

But if there is hope, it lies in the fact that science and technology can be intertwined with the sacred mystical path, which is also a spiritual and mythical path. They may be intertwined as they were in the beginning when science and mythology were intertwined, joined together. If there is a bridge to bring us back together again, it is in the form of water. Water is mankind's hope for the future. So let me speak about that.

Science has entered another archetype or model. Hopi myth has always said this, that man is part of the water cycle. Mankind is one with nature; we are inseparable. We are connected with all living things, all forms of life, and not just on Earth, but in the entire universe, the cosmos or orderly and harmonious universe. We are part of that. We are like seeds from the universe, seeds from the stars. And these seeds have memory. They know that human beings are part of water. Water connects us to everything, to the islands, the vast continents, and the oceans. The sixth direction is the cosmos, the dwelling of what Hopis call the Cloud People. That is where we all go when we leave our physical body on Earth. The water in our bodies evaporates and goes upwards, to the home of the Cloud

People. We take a rest there, but then we always return. We come back in the form of rain and snow. This gives water to all living things, to animals, insects and plants. We fill up the rivers, the lakes, the seas and the aquiferous regions of our world. This is our eternal journey back to the sea. And when we reach at last the sea, we return as clouds and as rain. This cycle is eternal, without end. And we are part of it. Water is indestructible; it is our link to the Great Spirit, the Creator. We are thus an integral part of the water cycle. We are not separate as western science believes. Hopis have always said that we are an important part of that eternal cycle. Hopis say we must join our hearts and our minds. Our prayers for rain vibrate and the Cloud People can feel these vibrations and they respond to our prayers. Hopis have been doing this for thousands of years. Water responds to our emotions and to our prayers. And thus the water is sacred. This is a fundamental Hopi belief which has existed for ages, and this powerful, sacred belief has enabled us to survive through the ages.

The Creator has given us this power, and so there is hope. Yet a change of heart is necessary. This can be used to create harmony anew on Earth, to bring holiness back to Earth because life is holy. But we need a change of heart to understand this and to use this gift *correctly. Mankind must have a mission and a goal in life. This should be our goal, but when we look around us at science, technology, pollution and the increasing destruction of our world, we see that we are not using it that way, the right way.*

Science and technology control our entire lives, they control our societies, they control the way we think and the way we behave. We bow down to them as gods. We do not know who the Great Spirit is anymore, we cannot feel His presence. The human race has to unite its energies, bring its hearts and minds together so we can get on the right path again. Today, we are on the path to destruction. This is the wrong path. The right path will bring harmony and peace back to Earth, before we embark on a path of total destruction. Hopis understand that we are on the wrong path, but our governors and leaders do not understand this because they are greedy and interested in control and power. But our Creator did not intend for us to live this way. He has repeatedly shown us that we have taken the wrong path. Peace, love and harmony must be brought back to Earth. That is our mission and it should be every human being's mission because that is the only way we can survive as a race. That is our hope. You, sitting there in the audience, you are our hope.

com/co

I met Claude and Chester in the Haight via a satirical writer by the name of Richard Brautigan, who was working on a novel with the uncanny title *Trout Fishing in America*. Rich was very witty but seemed to be a little shaken by a love relationship that wasn't exactly going the way he wanted it to. Claude Hayward had been living in San Francisco with his girlfriend since the fall of 1966, when things were really accelerating in the City and the neighborhood. He had worked for the *Los Angeles Free Press* in LA and found a job in San Francisco as advertising manager for *Sunday Ramparts*, a popular but struggling weekly created by the iconoclastic Warren Hinckle, executive editor of *Ramparts*. Chester Anderson arrived in San Francisco in early January 1967. Chester was a Greenwich Village poet, gifted musician and science fiction writer. Claude and Chester were living together on Duboce Avenue when I met them. Rich told me where their pad was and suggested that I pay them a call. He said they were really cool and into what was happening in the Haight-Ashbury, and would be glad to show me what they were doing as far as publishing is concerned. They had a really good mimeograph machine to tell everybody about their hopes and plans. They called their modest company com/co, which stands for the Communication Company.

Claude and Chester announced the creation of their company with a widely distributed flyer in the Haight.

The Communication Company
Haight/Ashbury
OUR POLICY
Love is communication.
OUR PLANS & HOPES
+ to provide quick & inexpensive printing service
for the hip community.
+ to print anything the Diggers want printed.
+ to do lots of community service printing.
+ to supplement The Oracle with a more or less daily
paper whenever Haight news justifies one, thereby
maybe adding perspective to The Chronicle's
fantasies.
+ to be outrageous pamphleteers.
+ to compete with the Establishment press for public

opinion.

+ to revive The Underground, old North Beach magazine of satire & commentary that was instrumental in ending a police harassment routine very like the present one.

+ to function as a Haight/Ashbury propaganda ministry, free lance if needs be.

+ to publish literature originating within this new minority.

+ to produce occasional incredibilities [*sic*] out of an unnatural fondness for either outrage or profit, as the case may be.

+ to do what we damn well please.

+ to keep up the payments on

OUR MAGNIFICENT MACHINES

* one brand-new Gestetner 366 silk-screen stencil duplicator.

* one absolutely amazing Gestefax electronic stencil cutter.

WITH WHICH WE CAN

+ print up to 10,000 nearly lithographic quality copies of almost anything we can wrap around our scanning drum.

+ on any kind of paper up to 8-1/2 by 14 inches (this being basically an office machine).

* with any kind of art, including half-tones.

* on both sides of the page.
+ in up to four colors with adequate registration
(office machine).
* with all manner of outrageous innovations.
* all in a very few hours.
   WE NEED ALL THE HELP WE CAN GET!
   WE NEED
+ printing orders.
+ Haight Street reporters.
* a whole lot of scripts for maybe publication.
+ writers for The Underground.
   claude & chester
626-2926
we deliver

I went to see Claude and Chester at 406 Duboce Avenue, and showed them a poem written by Brautigan as a form of introduction. I found Claude, a long-haired freak in his early twenties, maintaining a Gestefax mimeograph machine in the apartment. Chester was working on some new stencils. I showed an interest in what they were doing, so they opened up to me right away. I could see they knew a thing or two about printing. We smoked a doobie together and then they started talking about their plans.

Claude was really enthusiastic about their machines

because they could print thousands of high quality copies with half-tones on both sides of the page. Chester, a guy in his mid-thirties, said he often ran the machines during the day and welcomed any help he could get, because he also liked to go rambling through the Haight-Ashbury in search of news. Claude said he was working for the *Sunday Ramparts*, which was sometimes a drag, but it was a steady income.

When I mentioned the *Oracle*, they didn't show much enthusiasm. Oh, they liked the artwork and some of the articles, but Claude and Chester were into something else. That was not their thing. They had a very different perception of news and publishing. One of the problems with the *Oracle*, they said, was that it wasn't printed very often. Claude and Chester liked to come out with simple broadsides and screeds. "Our main goal is to spread information in the Haight-Ashbury, certainly not to dazzle our readers with sophisticated layouts and rainbow colors," they said. "We're living in a global village," said Claude, "and the medium is the message. It's impossible to know anything about social change in the world if you don't know that the media shape us because they are extensions of our faculties. Look at the way TV has changed society. The giant media corporations manipulate us and monopolize our senses. Com/co was created to give people back their basic rights, or at least a few of them."

They said they knew all the Diggers and they printed a lot of stuff for them. And because they were associated with the Diggers, their fliers and broadsides were always free. They didn't work for profit. Chester Anderson was quick to add, "We use quite a bit of material: paper, stencils, different colors of ink, and other materials. Some of it can get pretty expensive, so we have to get the money somewhere."

When I asked what Digger broadsides they had printed, they both ran off a list of names such as "Money Is an Unnecessary Evil" and "What Part of the Day Do You Spend Running." They said they printed some important stuff for Richard Brautigan, too. "Rich is going to be a legendary writer some day. Some important publishing houses are interested in his works, and we do what we can to make his name and his writings well-known in the Haight-Ashbury. We've printed *All Watched Over by Machines of Loving Grace,"* said Chester.

"Someday people will be real happy to find one of his original works printed by us," said Claude.

"As for the Diggers, they're good people, but some of them are a little pushy and possessive. We like to print what *we* like to print, without being told what to do," added Chester in his outspoken manner.

I thanked them for what they taught me and said I'd come around some day to help them out it they needed it. They told me I could come around whenever I wanted to, and that extra help was always nice to have.

17

Morningstar

Lou Gottlieb owned the property of Morningstar, a hippie commune north of San Francisco in Sonoma County, sprawling across thirty fantastic acres. It was a perfect place to get back to the land because the environment was unbelievably breathtaking, with redwood trees, an apple orchard, a chicken farm, houses and enough open country to please any naturalist.

Lou was in his forties and had gained fame by playing with The Limeliters trio. He was the mouthpiece for the group because of his friendly contact with audiences, his sense of humor and his wit. He had, in fact, analyzed jokes and affirmed that the best jokes had to have several parts: a premise, a punch line, a snapper, and, if you're lucky, a capper. One of his popular jokes went like this: I have a marvelous accident policy. If I'm ever bitten by a giraffe on the Golden Gate Bridge, I get $27.50 a week while I'm off work, but . . . I have to be pregnant at the time, and . . .

so does the giraffe! If you can make 'em laugh, half your battle is already won. Lou had a Ph.D. in musicology from U. C. Berkeley, so when it came to music, he knew his stuff. He had also played in clubs as a jazz pianist and arranged music for the Kingston Trio, one of the most popular folk groups in the entire country.

Lou got together with Glenn Yarbrough on guitar, Alex Hassilev on banjo and formed a folk trio. Lou played bass. Still without a name for the group when they premiered in Aspen, Colorado, they decided to call themselves The Limeliters, after the club called The Limelite.

Soon the trio headed for San Francisco, epicenter of the folk music scene at the time, where they played at the renowned hungry i, a nightclub in North Beach (later in Ghirardelli Square), famous for its stand-up comedians and music. As a matter of fact, the Kingston Trio and The Limeliters both recorded albums there.

The Limeliters were a tight musical group with a lot of positive energy, and they became an instant hit with audiences and talent scouts. Unlike many bands they were offered several recording contracts right off the bat, and they followed up with top-selling albums one after the other. They performed on a number of television shows, too, and made a hell of a lot of money advertising *Coca-Cola* and cigarettes.

Lou was living in San Francisco and working for the *San Francisco Chronicle* as a music critic. The job didn't last too long though, because he felt he didn't have enough freedom of expression and that editors at the paper were trying to force their opinions on him. The positive side of the job was that it got him in touch with the revolutionary music scene in the City and people like Stewart Brand, Ramón Sender, Chet Helms, Ben Jacopetti, Bill Graham and a host of others. Sender and his girlfriend Gina Stillman moved to Morningstar and stayed there on a permanent basis. Ben Jacopetti and his wife Rain also moved up to the ranch, and so did Lou Gottlieb. Word got around fast and acid heads and freaks saw it as an alternative to San Francisco and the Haight-Ashbury, which was going through some heavy changes. It seems the name "Morning Star Ranch" was inherited from the former owner's devotion to Christianity and the Virgin Mary. Somebody found old bills and letters with that name on it, and because Lou and the growing community liked its vibrations, decided to keep it.

Spirituality was seen as a vital aspect of Sonoma County, once inhabited by Native Americans, and the burgeoning commune was quickly inhabited by seekers who sought to unravel some of the mysteries of existence, something they had been initiated into by lysergic acid diethylamide. The first members of the commune were well-versed in the teachings of Zen masters and oriental sages like Aurobindo, Lama Govinda, Peter Ouspensky, George Gurdjieff and others.

A typical day would consist of hatha yoga, meditation and the reading of spiritual texts. Weather permitting, the activities were done in the open air. Some began using the word *ashram* to describe Morningstar when speaking about it to others.

When I went to Morningstar, I was met by Lou.

"Hey Lou," I said enthusiastically, "I've heard so much about this place that I needed to see it with my own eyes."

"Pilgrim," he replied, "I assume you know that we deny access to no one here at Morningstar. If you are lucky, you'll learn to do nothing here, something I'd like to learn how to do myself. We need to shut off our brains so we can achieve a higher state of consciousness. Now we have learned that LSD is a facet of the divine experience, and should, if we're not too stupid, be used to reveal the divine. LSD, as we at Morningstar are well aware, is a mystical transport that Saint Theresa and Saint John wrote about. They wrote about such things because they were interested in existence and the lives of their brothers and sisters. So if you deny yourself that extraordinary consciousness, what can I say? You must be a fool!

"So what's the goal of the commune?" I asked.

"What you are witnessing here at Morningstar is a sort of test, if you will, of society of the future, in which leisure will become obligatory. It's coming fast, like an avalanche, and there's no stopping it because of cybernation, the automatic control of processes in manufacturing by computers. Cybernetics, as you may already know, comes from the Greek word *kybernetes*, which essentially means *pilot* or *governor*. In the very near future, the goods and services that twentieth century society demands will be performed in a fraction of the time it takes to perform them today. As a result we're going to have massive compulsory leisure. This is already the case in the Haight-Ashbury where the hippies are turning on, tuning in and dropping out. They are the first wave of people produced by cybernetic industry and they are technologically unemployable. That means that you got a job, but you've been hearing voices saying: "A machine can do your job a lot better than you can." That's the beginning of the psychological preparation for dropping out.

"The people you see here at Morningstar have dropped out. They've been summoned, so to speak, by the land. And it's easy to get the ball rolling; all you have to do is buy some land and deny access to nobody. *Deny access to it to nobody.* That's my personal advice to people who own land. And bingo! The land will do the rest. It will call those who are best suited to make it beautiful. That's what the Indians did for thousands of years right here on this very same spot, and everything worked out well enough. There was no massive pollution as there is today. But then the natural harmony of the universe was disrupted because cau-ca-soids seized the land to make money. So, again, I'd say that what we're doing here is a sort of trial operation of the way people are going to live in the very near future. We've even called upon my old *alma mater*, U. C. Berkeley, to help in designing Morningstar. As I look around I'm always amazed by the diversity we see here today. Some are drawn to our gardens, while others are interested in putting together their own homes. Still, many I think need to learn how to do nothing. That's something I'd like to know how to do. To do nothing."

In the beginning of the beginning, let's say early 1967, there were just a few people living at Morningstar. But then the Diggers came around and said, "Well, you know, we're expecting a million crazy hippies this summer 'cause everyone is blabbin' about the Summer of Love; so can we take all your apples?"

Now it wasn't really a question, it was more like "What will you do if we take all your apples?" Next thing he knew, the Diggers were printing thousands of broadsides telling people in the Haight-Ashbury that the Digger Farm, more appropriately called Morningstar, was open and free, and so everyone knew how to get there. Some Diggers were sly when it came to expropriating property. The result was to be expected: waves upon waves of young people, many of which were destitute, showing up at the commune to live, get stoned and be fed.

When I was there for a few days, though never planning on staying, the weather was bright and sunny, so a lot of people were lightly dressed; the guys took off their shirts and quite a few of the girls, though not all of them, were nude. It didn't annoy anyone on the property, and seemed to fit in quite naturally. The problem was with the locals who had about as much empathy for the hippies as the Governor, the Mayor or the local Sheriff.

Morningstar was newsworthy and reporters focused on the things that sold papers: sex, psychedelics and nudity. Lou Gottlieb was not a stickler for rules, adhering more to the sixties ideals of *do your own thing* or *whatever turns you on*. People at the commune *were* doing their own thing, and some of them were minors and runaways. When some adolescent girls were treated for fungal infections of the vagina, the physicians called the cops and the serious hassles began.

Morningstar gave the impression of being *untamed*, though not in a negative sense. Vegetables were grown for eating and apples were produced in abundance, but there were a lot of weeds and tall grass growing everywhere. Nobody was interested in keeping the place immaculate, and that included Lou who, over the years, had considerably changed his ideas about tidiness and cleanliness. Who knows, maybe even defecating in the garden (of Eden) was a good thing, an expression of freedom. But the shit hit the fan rather than the garden.

Lou firmly believed in the sacred truth of the open land. He always defended that principle as a declaration of faith. In his states of higher consciousness, when the unity of existence presented itself as an epiphany, he understood that *land-access-to-which-is-denied-no-one* was the will of God, or for those who have problems with that word, the Eternal. Let the land decide who it wants to stay as a tribe. Might not such a premise provide the sanctuary so desperately sought by the technologically unemployed denizens of America's crumbling cities?

As I left Morningstar at dawn, I could not help but admire Lou's dream. He was a visionary. But like most visionaries, his visions would not be shared by the majority of Americans. I was sure that the hassles that were beginning for the commune would simply not go away, because those in positions of authority would not rest until they had destroyed his vision. Middle America simply could not ignore those who unabashedly rejected *their* dream, consumer values and *Leave it to Beaver*.

18

Plans for the Future

One evening I turned on my radio to see if I could find something interesting to listen to. It was an old radio that was badly broken and gave off a buzzing sound when the volume was turned up too high. I'd replaced the broken antenna with a metal clothes hanger. It wasn't particularly pleasing to the eye, but it usually worked and allowed me to tune in to the FM stations in the area. I'd stopped listening to AM radio because the programs were so shitty and the advertisements were a drag. As I was turning the dial I came across a fuzzy voice talking about the phoniness of society. It apparently wasn't on any station that I usually listened to. I couldn't tell when the discussion had begun, but it was already in progress and seemed to be broadcast before a live audience.

"[…] so it seems to me that we're all more or less phonies. (laughter) Now before you get excited, what

I'm specifically referring to is how the ego is a hoax, notwithstanding its iron grip on our lives. The ego hoax is a gift from our parents to all of us when we were children, before our rational minds were capable of questioning the lies we are forced to ingest in our youth.

"Society tells us that we are all different and that as unique individuals we are separate from the world around us. Human beings are creatures of habit and conditioning plays an essential role in our lives. We are conditioned by those who dominate us: our parents, teachers, priests, doctors, neighbors, friends, bosses, associates and everyone else to accept the idea that we are all separate and unique, just as they have accepted it as fact. Now the reason is quite simple: it helps us to function in society by not creating too much of a commotion.

"Thus hoodwinked, or shall I say swindled, rather than accomplishing what we've been told is our *unique* role in life, we are greatly frustrated in our attempts to achieve our goals. The frustration comes from the fact that we our unique individuals in a hostile, alien universe. Faced with what is an inherent conflict between ourselves and the world around us, we have attempted to dominate and conquer the natural world, as one might a recalcitrant mistress. (tittering in the audience)

"You may not be aware of the fact, but the Earth was once considered a living organism, and although its organs had specific functions, they served the entire body. In this sense rivers were compared to human veins. They flow from the mountains to the seas and oceans, like the blood which flows in our circulatory system to and from the heart. But this perception of our planet as a living organism changed with the development of science.

"Francis Bacon, of the sixteenth and seventeenth centuries, had a different perception of nature. For him it was not a living organism at all, but a sort of machine to be controlled and used by mankind. Taking advantage of nature was no longer seen as something iniquitous, but rather as a means of scientific progress towards a positive good.

"Of course this is absurd. We've been trying to dominate nature for centuries in the name of social, scientific or economic progress, but all we've done is to pollute the air, the water and the soil, to such an extent that some parts of the world have become uninhabitable. In spite of the spoliation of nature, we persist as before. So we've failed with nature, but we've also failed with our own lives. Although we fail today, we believe, or are led to believe, that we will succeed at sometime in the future; and if not ourselves, then our children or grandchildren. The result of these erroneous beliefs is that we forget about living in the present. We are conditioned to live for the future when all our impossible dreams will at last come true. Like Dorothy in *The Wizard of Oz*, we dream of flying over the rainbow. (laughter) But the rainbow in question keeps eluding us as it recedes from us, as assuredly as some men's hairlines recede as they get older. (laughter) We are trying to grasp a mirage, an illusion and a phantom.

"The consequence of all this foolishness is that we forget how to live in the present, which is the only way that real human beings can live. Now I ask you to think about it. If we are unable to really live in the present, in other words enjoy what we are doing now and achieve some sort of satisfaction from the fruits of our labor, will it be possible to live fully and achieve satisfaction in the future? (voices heard in the audience) Well of course not. If the present is a fraud, the future will be a fraud, too. So if we are incapable of living in the present because we are aiming our sights at the future, we are being suckered into accepting something that we don't really want. We are being cheated out of our happiness right here and now in the eternal present. So I ask you, what is the point of making plans for a future you won't be able to derive any satisfaction from?

When you get to the future, there will be another one after it, and another, and another, and so on forever and ever. In short, your train will never get to the station.

"If you think about it, everything we learn in school is like that, too. We are never taught to enjoy the present in the here and now, but to set our sights on that ultimate goal somewhere over the rainbow where bluebirds fly, whether we live in Kansas or not. (laughter) So all our lives we fight to be the top dog, to climb the social and economic ladder. And if you're really clever (Ha! Ha!), you'll invest in your retirement so that when you finally get to that bright shiny future you'll be sitting on a pot of gold. But guess what? When you get there, you realize that it's too late! You've got blood so tired that even Geritol can't help you, (laughter) heart disease, false teeth, a bald head, you're hard of hearing and you can't *get on up* as James Brown says. . . . (gales of laughter) In short, you're a miserable wreck. See what I mean? That future is a hoax, an imposter. When you should have been enjoying yourself in the here and now, you were planning for the future; and now that the future has finally arrived, you're thinking about the past and how you screwed up your life. (laughter)

"Now things could have been a hell of a lot different, mind you, if you had been able to live your life as if it were a game. Imagine how much different life could be if we didn't have all this ruthless, psychotic competition. If our work at school or on the job was really fun, like riding a bicycle on a warm summer day, winning at blackjack, going on a hike in the country, or dancing the cha-cha-cha with your lover, our lives would have been a lot less miserable. But as you can see, we have been *conditioned* to accept the fraud. Our Puritan work ethic has taught us that work can *never* be something you enjoy. When you work it must somehow be disagreeable. There can be no shenanigans at the workplace. Play, on the other hand, can be enjoyable. Now here's the capper. Our work is so monotonous and boring that they have to pay us to do it, or bring in *braceros* from Mexico because nobody else wants to do it. (noise in the audience) The point I'm making, you see, is that we don't do the work because we *enjoy* it, but because we're *paid* to do it. That's because almost everything in our society is based on money. And that's what the hippies in the Haight-Ashbury object to. If it's not *far out* and *groovy*, they avoid it as they would westerns with Ronald Reagan acting in them. (guffaws) The hippies don't want to serve hamburgers, work on an assembly line or sell vacuum cleaners, because they have to enjoy their work, whatever that may be. The problem is that when money is involved, we probably won't enjoy what we're doing. Time is money, right? I can see a lot of you shaking your heads. So you've got to work quickly. You can't take your time to make something really nice. Most people like to eat, but don't want to take the time to cook a tasty meal or don't have the time to cook. So they eat spaghetti in a can (he says chuckling). Now that may make Chef Boy-ar-dee happy, but what about you? Building contractors make a lot of money selling houses, but the houses they sell all look the same and are made of ticky-tacky, like in the song by Pete Seeger. The architects can't take the time to design beautiful, comfortable homes, because that would take too long. And it's the same thing wherever you go. Journalists don't have the time to write interesting, well-documented stories, so they take shortcuts, using sensationalism to appeal to their readers. And look at some of the paintings they put in museums today. They look like somebody threw the canned spaghetti at the canvas. And apart from the hippies in the Haight-Ashbury, who goes to a concert to listen to music? For that matter, who listens to music at home? Oh, I know, some do, but most people are watching the garbage they put on television to brainwash us into accepting the system, which deep down inside we all loathe because we know how fake it all is.

"Now this may surprise some of you, but contrary to popular belief, there are not too many genuine materialists anymore. In fact the word is a misnomer, because the material objects in question are pure junk. But why is that? That's because people don't enjoy their work. The goal of their work is not the final product, but the money they get paid to make the shoddy merchandise that keeps the economy stumbling along the rocky road to chaos. When I was working my way through college, I once worked at a factory that made water heaters. We had to work very fast on the assembly line to get a certain number of water heaters assembled every day. The guy I was working with wanted to work real fast, but he was cutting the holes in the metal sheets in the wrong places because we were going so fast. As a result, the water heaters couldn't be assembled properly. We were just working fast to get a bonus, not to make good water heaters.

"Since the goal of work is money and not quality products, all sorts of gimmicks are used to fool customers into thinking they're getting something really great, when in reality it's a pile of horse shit. (laughter) The reality, which people hate to hear by the way, is that most of the so-called material pleasures that people are conditioned to want on television and in advertising are just *illusions* of material pleasure. We're sold holograms of attractiveness and happiness, not the real thing, because the object is to make money, not to make quality products that last. That is the sad reality of material goods in our country today. Planned obsolescence is also part of the strategy. We're all like Willy Loman in *Death of a Salesman:* in a race with the junkyard. No civilization based on products falling apart and contaminating the environment can last. Vance Packard warned us about this waste . . . (A loud buzzing sound on the radio drowns out the speaker's voice and ends the broadcast.)

At that point I shut off the radio. Was this guy serious? I asked myself, or was he just putting on a show. His references to Chef Boy-ar-dee and botched water heaters got good laughs from the audience. Imagery of chefs with thick foreign accents wearing the customary toque flashed through my mind as I struggled to see how my perceptions of reality, my attitudes and relationships had been conditioned. Hare Krishna worshippers had a temple in the Haight and I'd briefly spoken to its members in the park. They claimed to have *dissolved* their ego and hence all conditioning, but I wasn't convinced: the shaved heads were a gimmick and the orange robes seemed to be worn as costumes by those who wanted the world to see how enlightened they were. Did Buddha try to eradicate his ego, or did he simply go beyond it? From what I'd read of Freud and other psychologists, they were not all in agreement about exactly what the ego is. A number of words associated with the word like *egocentric*, *egoism*, *egotist* or *ego trip* came to mind. I could see how these negative attitudes could be an obstacle to healthy social behavior.

I wondered, too, if we Westerners truly understand what Eastern religions meant by selflessness. Perhaps it was possible to perceive our true nature without trying to decapitate the ego, as though it were an enemy. And then I began thinking about my sense of *volition*. It did not seem to me that all our desires were bad. How could desiring to live in harmony with the universe (if that's possible) be bad, or desiring to end ignorance, exploitation, domination, war, pollution and a hundred other evils that have contaminated our world for so long be bad? The more I thought about it, the more I was confronted with questions that loomed before me like an impenetrable mountain range.

19

Money

As I was leafing through my Funk and Wagnalls the other day I was amazed by how many idioms there are about money in our language: *a fool and his money are soon parted, a quick buck, money talks, a high roller, blood money, born with a silver spoon in one's mouth, born into money, bring home the bacon, a cash cow, a cheapskate, daylight robbery, dough, from rags to riches, funny money, ride the gravy train, hard cash, to have sticky fingers, he who pays the piper calls the tune, head over heels in debt, to get the lion's share of the money, money doesn't grow on trees, money isn't everything, money makes the world go around, the other side of the coin, to pay a king's ransom, to pay an arm and a leg, to pay through the nose, to be a penny-pincher, to pour money down the drain, to throw money out the window, to put one's money where one's mouth is, to save money for a rainy day, to be strapped for cash, the best things in life are free, to be broke, to cook the books, to cut corners, to earn a living, to get off scot-free, to give somebody a run for their money, to go bust, to go for broke, to burn a hole in one's pocket, to laugh all the way to the bank, spare change, to panhandle, to take someone to the cleaners, to throw money around, dirty money, to turn up like a bad penny, to put your two cents in. . . .* There are dozens more, but I'll stop here.

The Holy Bible has a lot to say about money, too:

"Keep your life free from love of money, and be content with what you have, for he has said, 'I will never leave you nor forsake you.'" (Hebrews 13:5)

"For the love of money is a root of all kinds of evils. It is through this craving that some have wandered away from the faith and pierced themselves with many pangs." (Timothy 6:10)

"The rich rules over the poor, and the borrower is the slave of the lender." (Proverbs 13:11)

"No one can serve two masters, for either he will hate the one and love the other, or he will be devoted to the one and despise the other. You cannot serve God and money." (Matthew 6:24)

"He who loves money will not be satisfied with money, nor he who loves wealth with his income; this also is vanity." (Ecclesiastes 5:10)

"And he said to them, 'Take care, and be on your guard against all covetousness, for one's life does not consist in the abundance of his possessions.'" (Luke 12:15)

"Do not lay up for yourselves treasures on earth, where moth and rust destroy and where thieves break in and steal, but lay up for yourselves treasures in heaven, where neither moth nor rust destroys and where thieves do not break in and steal. For where your treasure is, there your heart will be also." (Matthew 6:19-21)

"Owe no one anything, except to love each other, for the one who loves another has fulfilled the law." (Romans 13:8).

Apart from their spiritual truths, these passages emphasize the profound importance of money in society. Western man has never known a world where money hasn't dominated his life and thoughts.

The Diggers of San Francisco often spoke about money, because the sages of Diggerism understood how it influenced human behavior. One of the texts printed by com/co and the Diggers was entitled "Money Is an Unnecessary Evil."

Money Is an Unnecessary Evil

It is addicting.

It is a temptation to the weak (most of the violent crimes of our city in some way involve money).

It can be hoarded, blocking the free flow of energy and the giant energy-hoards of Montgomery Street will soon give rise to a sudden and thus explosive release of this trapped energy, causing much pain and chaos.

As part of the city's campaign to stem the causes of violence the San Francisco Diggers announce a 30 day period beginning now during which all responsible citizens are asked to turn in their money. No questions will be asked.

Bring money to your local Digger for free distribution to all. The Diggers will then liberate its energy according to the style of whoever receives it.

Like many of the Diggers' texts, humor and satire were intertwined with serious elements. The Diggers had high hopes of changing people's motivations, but they certainly didn't expect long lines of capitalists yearning to *liberate* their money. What I noticed right off the bat was how money is associated with negative values in the text. It is a "temptation to the weak," it is a cause of violent crime, it is "hoarded," it blocks energy, it causes "much pain and chaos."

Diggers let out a war whoop when they felt some were trying to profit off the counterculture in the Haight-Ashbury, and they were a force to be reckoned with because they had their own media with com/co, were tight with the Hell's Angels, and were capable of mobilizing hundreds or thousands of hippies to support them.

The Love Conspiracy Commune was presenting the First Annual Love Circus at Winterland and featuring Love, the Grateful Dead, Moby Grape, Loading Zone and the Blue Crumb Truck Factory, the last group I'd never heard of. Other attractions included a lightshow and body and face painting, but there was a hitch. Tickets sold for $3.50. A lot of people didn't have three dollars and fifty cents to see a rock concert, or even $1.50. The Diggers were pissed off because they felt the ticket price was inflationary and that people were selling out. They moved into action quickly and picketed the show, arguing that events in the Haight-Ashbury such as the Human Be-In and The Invisible Circus were free. Of course The Invisible Circus was a fiasco, but that was something else. Personally, I thought it was all a tempest in a teacup . . . or maybe a tempest in a hash pipe.

Anyhow, the Love Conspiracy Commune replied by contacting com/co and getting a response printed up, promising to help the picketers out. Jerry Garcia and the Grateful Dead said they wouldn't perform unless the picketers could see the show for free. Some people actually did get in for free, but then the doors were closed, supposedly because non-picketers were taking advantage of the opportunity to see a free show. Anyway, from then on, I noticed that prices at the Fillmore and Winterland continued to rise.

Bill Graham knew the Diggers, at least some of them. He'd met Emmet Grogan, Peter Coyote, Peter Berg and a few others. Bill grew up the hard way, the *really* hard way, so he had respect for the street-wise group. The Diggers didn't really like having to go to Graham to organize something, but sometimes Bill was indispensable. He was at the hub of the music scene in the Haight.

Now it should be understood that the Diggers, at least some of the ones I knew, were not mild-mannered hippies. Any idea associating them to the Salvation Army is as far from the truth as you can get. They were strong-willed and did whatever they thought was necessary to get what they wanted, and they sometimes had the Hell's Angels on their side.

The Diggers were playing with people's minds in the sense that they wanted to change their way of thinking and their behavior. If you have ever tried to do that you know that people don't change easily. The Diggers wanted people to question what they were doing with their lives, to see how money perverts relationships and to realize that they are always being exploited.

They could see that most people are slaves to their culture and to their personal identity. *Free*, a key word in Digger diction, means that your ego doesn't take credit for what you do to help your brothers and sisters. If you get your picture in the newspaper and people praise you for it, then it isn't *free* at all, because you're getting credit for it.

If you were really crazy, and God knows there were some *really* crazy dudes in the Diggers and the Haight, you might put a table on the freeway where people could stop and find out what was going on. The Diggers must have loved the word *freeway* and what it represented because you didn't have to pay to drive your car on it.

The subtext was what was really important. It was all about revolution, which is to say *change*. When change was happening, that was great because it was a form of revolution.

There was this guy called Sweet William–I think his real name was Fritsch. He was a Hell's Angel and he associated with the Diggers. He was intimidating because of his attitude and because of the way he talked and dressed. Anyway, he went with Peter Berg to see Bill Graham to ask for money. That's the only reason they went to see Graham, to get some money out of him. I wasn't there, I don't know what was said, but the message must have been clear because Bill just took out his checkbook and signed a check for five hundred dollars. Now Bill wasn't a punk. He could have stonewalled if he'd chosen too, but he probably didn't want any problems with those roughs either. He probably figured that $500 would be cheap compared to the trouble those cats could give him if they wanted to. The Diggers didn't *really* like Graham because he was making good money with his shows at the Fillmore. It seems to me that the Diggers kind of went overboard that way with the HIP merchants. They didn't like the merchants on Haight Street because they were selling stuff to make a living. But in reality, none of them were really prosperous, and some of them, like the Psychedelic Shop, were in debt for thousands of dollars that they would never pay off. One could say that if the Diggers were really against people making money, then they should have gone after the big fish, like the mafia, the Aliotos and some of those guys. But it's always easier to pick on the little people who don't know how to defend themselves. The shops on Haight Street were small fry. They were nothing compared to the high rollers in North Beach and Montgomery Street. The Diggers and the tough bikers didn't fuck with those dudes because they knew they were way out of their league and that they'd be spending time in jail, or even worse, if they messed around with them. I couldn't imagine the mafia wasting time with hippies, bikers or anybody else that got in their way.

20

The Human Be-In

The people at the *Oracle* said that Allen Cohen and Michael Bowen had the idea for the Be-In in Golden Gate Park, which finally took place on 14 January 1967. Bowen was an artist and a mystic who knew a lot of *heavy* people and almost everyone of consequence in the Haight-Ashbury. He was older than a lot of us, representing the generation born in the thirties. Of course he knew Timothy Leary and his sidekick Richard Alpert; in fact, he was busted at Millbrook in 1965, a fact which made him an immediate success in the neighborhood. Allen Cohen was the guy who had the idea for the *Oracle*. Some people claimed that Bowen's so-called guru in Cuernavaca, Mexico, was indirectly related to the Agency, but nobody seemed to know too much about that. The two visionaries met at Mike's apartment at the corner of Masonic and Haight Street and played with the idea of a large gathering in Golden Gate Park, with prominent figures of the counterculture articulating their wisdom, poets reading their works, bands playing rock music, and people turning on to Owsley's latest brew.

The press conference at the Print Mint on Haight Street was a big to-do, with journalists and cameramen from the local media guzzling the latest scoop from the Haight. A large crowd was outside in the street hoping to get a peek inside, but no one was allowed to enter, and there wasn't any room anyway. Hippie bigwigs were politely on hand to answer any questions the mainstream news outlets might have about what was billed as "a gathering of the tribes." Since radicals were turning on to pot and acid, some figured that a little cooperation between Berkeley and the Haight-Ashbury would result in greater social and political influence. At least that was the optimistic view.

It seems some high caliber astrologers had been contacted to look into the stars to find a good date for the psychedelic happening. Several of those were contributing articles to the *Oracle*.

I saw three far out posters for the Human Be-In, but maybe there were more. They were made by Rick Griffin, a gifted artist from Southern California who had moved up north, and Michael Bowen. Griffin's poster with a Native American on horseback seemed well-suited for the event. The work by Bowen, Stanley

Mouse and Casey Sonnabend with the *sadhu* was outta sight, too, I thought.

Saturday morning I was up at dawn. "It's going to be a groovy day," I said to myself. I did some yoga and a few exercises and then made myself some strong cappuccino the way I like it. There was no grass to be found, but I was pretty sure there'd be plenty on hand in the park. Knowing there'd be a large gathering, I got to the Polo Field early to check out the scene, but I didn't want to get squeezed up against a platform like a sardine in a can. I remembered the posters saying everything would start at one.

The organizers were attentive to symbols and didn't leave anything to chance. I saw Ginsberg and Snyder in a small group of people walking around the area in a somewhat solemn manner. At the time, I didn't know what they were doing, but the Thelin brothers told me that they were performing a sacred ritual to purify the space and ward off demonic spirits and bad vibes. Jay said the ceremony is called *pradakshina*. Satanists had visited the field the night before, leaving signs of their intent to disturb the mellow vibrations.

Gary Snyder opened the event by blowing on a conch. I thought he did that pretty well, because it takes some practice to get a decent sound out of the shell. Of course that's a very symbolic act, too, because the conch shell is associated with Vishnu, the Hindu god called the Protector. When you hear the trumpeting of the shell, it's supposed to chase away illusions and evil spirits.

Next on the program was Ginsberg, who led the crowd in a healing mantra: *Hari om namah shivaya*. He wanted the audience to participate, but most were too inhibited to do that; or maybe they just came to see a show.

"Welcome to the first manifestation of the Brave New World," said a voice from the stage. I had to admit that I didn't understand what he was suggesting. For me it was a direct reference to Aldous Huxley's *Brave New World*. Huxley, a British author who'd used psychedelics before most people, depicts a nightmarish dictatorship in his novel, where the different castes are biologically and psychologically conditioned from birth. They use soma, a drug that represses consciousness. In the Brave New World of the future nobody wants to change anything at all, and religion has become a grotesque parody.

Lenore Kandel was at the Be-In and it was her birthday. Everyone had fun singing "Happy Birthday" to her off-key, and she seemed a little sheepish when they did. She spoke about Buddha, saying he would reach everyone through love, not through his doctrine or religious teachings. Maitrcya, she said, would not be born in one physical body, but in the large gathering that had assembled in the Polo Field. Was she invoking the divinity in man?

The sights around me were truly amazing. I'd never seen such a large crowd in Golden Gate Park. Tens of thousands of people were having fun in the unusually mild January weather. Everything was vibrating with lights and colors. Marijuana was being smoked freely because the police couldn't do anything about it. How do you arrest 30,000 people? If you were in the back, you couldn't hear what was being said, because the sound system wasn't tops, though it didn't really seem to matter that much.

Timothy Leary was there, dressed in white pajamas and beads. He'd arrived in the Bay Area to perform his "Death of the Mind" shows. "Turn on, tune in and drop out . . . drop out of college, drop out of graduate school, drop out of junior executive, drop out of senior executive, turn on tune in, drop out," he said. But people hadn't come to listen to Tim's slogans. Most just wanted to listen to the bands.

Jerry Rubin represented the radicals from Berkeley. He was awkward and seemed out of place. He blundered through a diatribe against the war machine in Washington D. C., but you could tell that people weren't really interested. Rubin said he'd recently been released from jail, but the crowd didn't understand why that was important.

The poets were there–Allen Ginsberg, Gary Snyder, Lenore Kandel Michael McClure, Lawrence Ferlinghetti, Lew Welch–but the Polo Field wasn't a good place to read poetry. Like the other speakers, the psychedelic celebrities were largely ignored.

Quite a few local bands were scheduled to play–the Dead, Quicksilver Messenger Service, Jefferson Airplane, the Loading Zone, Sir Douglas Quintet, Big Brother, Country Joe and the Fish–but I didn't see them all perform on stage.

Augustus Owsley Stanley III was handing out his latest batch called White Lightning, and the Diggers were handing out sandwiches with LSD in the mayonnaise. That explains why a lot of people were so stoned at the Be-In.

One thing that stood out in my mind was the diversity. The Gathering of the Tribes was not a freak show–all kinds of people were in the crowd and you could identify three or maybe even four generations. Most of the guys had average-length hair and some dudes looked like they were from the financial district. And there were a lot of toddlers walking around nude; they didn't seem to be unhappy or afraid. Quite a few couples were pushing strollers that were ornamented with flowers, bells, balloons all the colors of the rainbow, or a God's eye (ojo de dios) that helps you to see the spiritual world.

Soap bubbles made with giant bubble wands and the happy sounds of flutes and jangling bells added to the festivities. The vibrations were idyllic. One girl in black swirled in place near the stage, probably annoying those around her, but nobody said anything out loud.

The Hell's Angels were in charge of lost children, and there were a few. The loud-speaker on the platform was used to make such announcements, giving a description of the child and its name if they knew it.

One particularly spectacular event was the parachutist who fell out of the sky from nowhere. "Where's the plane? Did you see a plane fly by?" people asked. The parachutist appeared like an angel descending from heaven. Was it a lifesaver? In William Golding's *Lord of the Flies*, it represented the children's fears. It was the "beast." At the Be-In it represented different things for different people, and some saw something magical in it.

As the happening ended, groups of people clasped hands to form chains, a common practice in the Haight-Ashbury, and frolicked in serpentine movement. Someone announced on the loudspeaker that it would be far out to clean up the litter left behind. Those of us who were still there picked it all up, because it was the right thing to do. We left the polo grounds immaculate, thus depriving City Hall of any opportunity to badmouth the hippies.

One could sense a feeling of wholeness and tranquility as the rivers of people left the area. "This is who we are. This is what we can do. Simply *being* can give a feeling of satisfaction, accomplishment and well-being." I shared that feeling, but I couldn't ignore another feeling: *Can it last?*

Issue number five of the *San Francisco Oracle* was published to advertise the Human Be-In. It was printed in early January and some 50,000 copies, an impressive number for an underground paper, were printed. Hundreds or thousands were given away for free, many at the Be-In. Colored ink (purple) was used for the first time. Allen Cohen, Ron Thelin and Steve Leiper edited the issue. Gabe Katz was art director and many more were involved in the publication, including Michael Bowen and Mouse Studios for artwork.

The goal was to promote the psychedelic revolution that was blossoming everywhere. The Hindu holy man on the front page became an icon of the counterculture. It was used by Bowen to make a poster for the Be-In because he believed the *sadhu* exemplified the spiritual motivations of the organizers. Whether the "gathering of the tribes" actually bridged the gap between Berkeley radicals and Hasbury hippies is open to debate. Everything is political, in one way or another, but not everyone has what it takes to become a political activist, and every political movement needs a strong sense of direction and long-term goals. It seemed to me that those things were lacking in the psychedelic counterculture.

Former Harvard psychologist and researcher Dick Alpert contributed an article entitled "Ees Setisoppo," which spells "See Opposites" backwards. Leary's former collaborator must have been stoned during the interview, which didn't help to make the text more coherent, but the *Oracle's* readers were probably not too interested in the niceties of composition.

A passage in Alpert's monologue that bothered me was about the death of a teenage hippie. Some people on acid were having a party up on the eighth floor of a building. One youth said he was going to jump out the window. Somebody said that was "cool," and so the guy jumped from the eighth floor. Someone told Alpert that that was "horrible." Alpert's response: "Well, what's so horrible about it?" Apparently he was thinking that since his life made a strong statement, everything was alright. Maybe I missed the point, but his reaction seemed terribly callous to me, especially since he advocated the use of LSD. Timothy Leary would have shown more empathy and compassion, I thought, because he emphasized the importance of *set* and *setting*. A person's particular (mind)set and the social and physical environment in which a person has a psychedelic experience are always important. Negative emotions and negative surroundings can have disastrous consequences for a person on an acid trip. The consequences of their acts in the physical world are not always clear to them when reality is difficult to define. The same could be said about people who drink too much alcohol. Tens of thousands of persons die every year because of alcohol, but the media are less interested in those deaths.

21

Chocolate George

Hell's Angel George Hendricks, better known as "Chocolate" George, was a well-known figure in the Haight-Ashbury, along with a number of other bikers in the motorcycle gang. I didn't know Chocolate George personally, but I'd seen him riding his Hog on Haight Street. He had been given that nickname because he drank chocolate milk.

George came into this world on 7 October 1932, and roared out of it on 24 August 1967, when he had a fatal accident at the corner of Haight and Shrader. I have no idea whose fault it was, but other bikers I'd seen riding had little regard for safety and the rules of the road. A lot of people learned later that for the last twelve years he'd been working for the Recreation Center for the Handicapped, handing out equipment and doing other stuff. His real profession was mechanic, a skill he used to keep his Harley rolling.

I heard a long-haired dude talking about him at the

funeral as though he knew him well. "Chocolate was a cool dude, man. You should o' seen the way he rode his hog, man. And like he was just thirty-four, ya know; and that's a shitty way to leave this friggin world, man. All the freaks I know loved Chocolate, and we'd turn him on to his favorite drink when we could. Like he was our brother, man. The asshole that hit him killed our brother. That ain't right man, ya know what I mean? That ain't right, man. Now I'm really fucked up now, ya see? 'Cause I dropped acid. Wow! and we gave Chocolate a grooooovy funeral. Like we heard some grooooovy music and got righteously fucked up, man. And that's cool, 'cause that was the way to say *adiós* to our brother, our brother Chocolate."

The funeral procession for George was at least four blocks long. Dozens of Hell's Angels rode down Dolores Street on their Harleys. The Daphne Funeral Home at 1 Church Street was packed with mourners, all bikers of course. The wake, which wasn't a wake, not in a traditional sense, anyway, was held in Lindley Meadow in Golden Gate Park. There were a lot of bikers there, and a lot of Hell's Angels. I stayed at a respectful distance, knowing that those dudes can be really unpredictable. The hippies were kept at a distance, too, but the hippie elite were rubbing elbows with the bikers.

Things started happening in the early afternoon. You could smell the pot everywhere and my guess is that people were dropping acid, too, though I couldn't see why they'd need it at a funeral. The bikers always had a lot of beer and cheap wine around wherever they went, and they were getting louder and rowdier as they got drunker and drunker.

Big Brother and the Holding Company was playing, and playing really loud. And when Janis started wailing "Bye, Bye Baby," the bikers went crazy, hooting and hollering and throwing stuff around. The Grateful Dead were there to play, too.

The Hell's Angels let everyone know they were the boss, but there were a number of biker gangs including the Gypsy Jokers and Satan Slaves. Some of the bikers got pissed off, as they tend to do when they're wiped out, and stomped some hippies who were getting in their way.

Ever since 1965, the gang had become an integral part of the neighborhood. Some of them spent a lot of time on Haight Street and were intimate with a few of the Diggers and the bands. At first glance this seemed to be a paradox because many weren't particularly emblematic of the peace and love scene, so I often wondered about this relationship. I guess camaraderie was part of it. The Diggers weren't hippies, so that connection must have been different.

As far as *love, violence* and *the relationship to the land* were concerned, the bikers and the freaks had different values, at least in theory. Hippies were opposed to violence and sometimes became victims themselves because of this creed. The violence of the bikers was as notorious as it was unpredictable. Similarly, hippies often spoke about love in the sense of brotherly love, tolerance and universal love. The hippie idea of getting back to nature also articulated a different perception of the environment, which in large part was borrowed from the Native Americans. The counterculture was opposed to all wars and particularly the War in Vietnam, but many bikers openly supported the war, were racists and physically and verbally attacked those who protested against the war. The Nazi emblems some of the bikers wore said a lot about their attitudes and behavior, too.

On the other hand, if one considered the ideas of deviant behavior, dropping out and freedom, some similarities probably did exist. Both bikers and hippies expressed attitudes of alienation from American society; both had *dropped out* in one way or another; both valued *doing your own thing,* to use the slogan of the time. Perhaps the bikers were drawn to the hippies because the flower children were easy to intimidate, although they liked to say they were protecting the Haight-Ashbury and the hippies. The bikers treated some of them as if they were pets, giving them orders and expecting immediate gratification of their demands. Ken Kesey was close to them for a while, but that seemed to change when he moved back to Oregon. Of course such comparisons are further complicated by the inevitable generalizations and stereotypes that result from establishing paradigms. Group behavior tends to be more predictable than individual acts. I'll sum it all up by saying unpredictability is as predictable among the biker gangs as the changing of the seasons.

22

Going Bananas for Bananatine

In the March 1967 issue of the *Berkeley Barb*, an underground paper created by Max Scherr, an unusual recipe was given for bananas: after freezing the banana peels, you create a pulp out of them, and then put the pulp in the oven until the mixture is dry enough to be smoked. The idea of the recipe was to get high by smoking banana peels. Supposedly, the rumor was spread by a friend of Country Joe and the Fish, the psychedelic band from Berkeley.

"Ha, Ha Ha" begins the article from the *Berkeley Barb*, published on 24 March 1967, Volume 4, Number 12, Issue 84, page 3. The article signed NF, affirms that hundreds of people got stoned in the Panhandle by smoking bananas. Now it's our turn, "Ha, Ha, Ha!" Some said the Diggers were also involved in the hoax. So what did they do? They scrounged one hundred pounds of bananas, scraped off the insides of the peels, added a little water, boiled it for two to three hours until it became a disgusting mess, spread the shit on cookie-sheets, and then dried it all in an oven until it was ready to smoke. "Ha, Ha, Ha!"

Scientists are able to verify if banana skins contain serotonin and norepinephrine or not. So if the gooshy mess oxidizes, it may produce bufotenine, supposedly a psychedelic substance.

Country Joe and the Fish said they had smoked banana skins and got stoned, which, however, would be hard to prove from a scientific standpoint because the band was already stoned out of their gourds when they tried the banana peels. Country Joe McDonald reportedly went all over Berkeley turning people on to banana peels; but Joe, it should be remembered, was fond of publicity stunts that helped to advertise himself, his band and their music. It seems that the band's manager, Eugene "ED" Denson, advised stoners to soak grass in banana oil for a super high. "Banana oil" was a euphemism of the older generation for bullshit! So people, it could be said, were up to their necks in *banana oil* at the time.

To put things in their proper perspective, it should be remembered that Donovan came out with a best-selling single entitled "Mellow Yellow" on Epic Records on October 22, 1966, which, by the way, was Timothy

Leary's birthday. Donovan wrote the song, played acoustic guitar and sang the lyrics. Probably not everyone knew at the time that the Beatle's Paul McCartney sang backup vocals for the single that was a huge success for Donovan Leitch.

It was rumored that the song was about smoking dried banana skins, thought to make people hallucinate. But that was not the case. Donovan's liner notes say that Country Joe McDonald was the source of the rumor which began in 1966. Donovan only learned about that a few weeks before the single was released. He made reference to an "electrical banana" in the song, but that had nothing to do with psychedelics. It was about a yellow vibrator. Seems he was reading the paper and saw an advert for a yellow dildo referred to as *mellow yellow*. Oh là là!

Meanwhile, the banana hysteria went all the way to Congress. On 12 May Representative Frank Thompson Jr. of New Jersey got involved in the hoax by proposing the Banana Labeling Act of 1967. Of course that was all a joke, too, but the law would have required producers to put stickers on the fruit that said "Caution: Banana Peel Smoking May Be Injurious to Your Health. Never put bananas in the refrigerator."

In a press release on 26 May 1967, the Food and Drug Administration felt it necessary to issue a disclaimer, stating that there were no "detectable quantities of known hallucinogenics" in the bananas they analyzed.

Publisher's note: For those who like Amsterdam, you'll be interested to know that Mellow Yellow, apparently the oldest coffee shop in the city, opened its doors in 1972. It's situated at Vijzelgracht 33, 1017 HN Amsterdam, and is recognizable by its familiar yellow and black façade.

I recall that a lot of my friends were going bananas for bananas as they sought a legal high. Freaks in the Haight-Ashbury were buying bananas, to such an extent, in fact, that Safeway was running out of them. But those jokers were a few bananas short of a bunch. Stoners were very meticulous in their efforts to follow the recipe to the letter, and people, myself included, smoked the dried pulp inside of the skins. As far as I can remember, no one got high on bananas; just a lot of banana oil thrown in with the rest of the bullshit. But at the same time, one had to admit that it said something about the psychedelic counterculture. It showed me that people would go to no small lengths to get stoned, which explains why there were some bad trips that weren't *all* psychological. Sometimes people were ingesting poison, or drugs that were cut with all kinds of garbage that your body can't deal with. And there was no way to really know what was in the stuff or how big of a dose you were taking.

23

Psychedelic Rangers

My friend Van had just returned from Mexico with some wild stories about psychedelic rangers and stoner gurus so I asked him to come over and lay it on me. There were still some Panama Red buds in my stash, so I rolled a joint with my rolling machine, because that works out better for me than trying to roll them myself, and waited for my friend to come. Van said he'd taken some acid, but smoked a joint with me anyway.

He'd heard about a crippled guru living near Cuernavaca, in a village called Tepoztlán. Somebody gave him the guru's phone number, so he was able to arrange a meeting with the guy, who seemed interested in Van because he lived in the Haight-Ashbury, was close to people in the Family Dog, and was eager to learn more about mysticism and the tarot. Van, with his usual stream of consciousness rap, said he was blown away by the beauty of the region.

Say man, you really gotta check out this groovy

place, 'cause I know you'll dig it, man. It's called the sacred valley of Tepoztlán. Wow! Like it's sublime, can you dig it? I visited the museo and the Mercado, and it's really cool. Like they sell all these fruits and vegetables that you've never even heard of before, man. I had a little trouble finding the dude's place at first. Por favor, ¿dónde vive el gurú? I asked. But then I ran into a couple of freaks who told me how to get there. By the way, the guru's name is Cooke, John Starr Cooke. A really mystical dude, you dig? When I got to his pad he was contemplating his tarot cards. And the weather was really groovy and the breeze was perfumed by all kinds of tropical flowers. There were even orange trees! Can you dig it man, fuckin' orange trees! Of course this is in the mountains, 'cause it's like more than 1,700 meters above sea level.

So, anyway, I met this bald dude with a goatee, and he had really piercing eyes, man. Like I felt he was looking right through me. I introduced myself and we drank some tea or something. John told me a little about himself, saying he had settled in Southern Mexico after leaving Carmel on the California coast. He said he liked the climate in Morelos and the groovy topography in Tepoztlán. There's this heavy mountain called El Tepozteco that towers above the town, and there's this really old pyramid where Aztec gods were worshipped by the natives. You dig what I'm sayin', man?

Anyway, this guru dude has all these mystical powers. He touched my forehead and I felt like I was stoned, like I was rushing on acid or something. John said he liked to see a lot of people, because that was all part of the changes that 'r' goin' down 'cause of the Aquarian Age. He called it the New Dawn. While I was there, he got a couple of phone calls. He said he got calls from people all 'round the world. I don't know, man, but this dude has this heavy persona, or aura. He told me he'd traveled all over in Northern Africa with his wife, looking for all kinds of mystical experiences. And there was this group of Sufis that John settled in with. They called him a saint and a healer, and said he could arouse shakti, the cosmic energy everywhere in the universe. But then he had a real bummer in Tangiers, man. I think he said it was in a bank or somethin'. He was waitin' in line to change some money, when he felt like his shoulders were being barbecued. Some asshole put a fuckin' scarf on his shoulders, man. And then he said he felt like some dude punched him in the fuckin' back. He doesn't know what they put in the scarf, but he said he became paralyzed after that, that he couldn't walk anymore. Can you believe this? This guru dude had even worked with L.

Ron Hubbard, ya know, the guy who created Dianetics and Scientology. Far out man . . . and he told me about Thetan, auditing, Xenu and the whole schmear. John even asked Hubbard for help, but like he was tied up in England, or somethin' and couldn't get away, so he sent an Australian dude, Jim Skelton, who was into the movement, but that didn't do any good. John tried to get help from other spiritual heavies, but that didn't do any good either.

Now ya know what's really groovy is that while he was in Carmel, John was introduced to Michael Bowen, you know him right? That artist dude living in the Haight. Bowen was blown away by this guru, completely blown away, man. Like they've been friends ever since they met. In Carmel Cooke created the New Tarot Deck for the Aquarian Age and was dropping acid every day. Can ya dig it? He was into alcohol, too. He's got all kinds of really heavy dudes lining up to meet him all the time, man. That's because he's into all kinds of heavy occult things. There was this one guy who did experiments for the American military. I think he said his name was Pewrich, or maybe Andrija Puharich, or somethin' like that. Later some guys told me that this guru knows dudes in the CIA, man, 'cause they were turned on to acid, too. There's all kinds of secret stuff related to this shit. I mean wow. . . . And there's this master plan to get people turned on to acid. I donno who developed it, but the dude in the wheelchair was part of it.

Van went on with his heavy rap and I wasn't sure if the acid or the Panama Red was doing the talking. Anyway, he explained who the Psychedelic Rangers were: a group of missionaries who were reportedly giving huge doses of acid to certain people to change their way of seeing things and win them over to the cause. Normally, an LSD trip involves a dose of about 100 to 250 milligrams, assuming one can be that precise. But much higher doses were apparently being given to some really essential people. I could imagine how people were reacting with the excessive doses. Michael Bowen, one of Cooke's protégés, was turning on entertainers, journalists and political figures like Jerry Rubin, who, with Abbie Hoffman, later became one of the leaders of the Yippies. A lot of the celebrities, if not all, criticized the United States for its lack of compassion, its greed and its aggressivity. There was obviously a political trip involved, but I didn't know how deep it went. One view was that the "free world" had to protect everyone else from communism.

But for many, including John Cooke, LSD could be used as a weapon against the darker forces of the material world. These people saw existence as a duality, a Manichaeism, so they had this view of good and evil, with the forces of good engaged in an eternal combat with the dark forces of iniquity. The field of battle was the human soul. It seems this war has been going on forever.

Michael Bowen was in constant communication with Cooke in Mexico to let him know what was happening in the Haight-Ashbury. The Haight was a special place, because people were seeing God, or so they said, and understanding the spiritual unity of the universe. One of the goals of the Psychedelic Rangers was to get important people stoned on LSD, so in this sense, acid was viewed as a tool for changing people's minds and behavior, or, to use another term, *recondition* people. In that sense, it was felt that happenings like the Human Be-in could bring about the salvation of humanity, provided that enough people got stoned on acid. Michael Bowen called John Cooke right after the Love Pageant Rally to see what could be done on a larger scale. The underground media was enthusiastic about such happenings, because they believed it was a good way of getting lots of people together, and that could ultimately change the *status quo*. The *Berkeley Barb*, the best selling underground paper in the Bay Area, advertised the Be-In on the front page to get as many people interested as possible. The Be-In would help to usher in a New Dawn for humanity, when the forces of darkness would yield to the forces of light, and harmony would return to the planet. Pollution, desecration and exploitation would end as people became one with the universal spirit. But it seems the plan somehow backfired, because hippies and radicals started to attack American hegemony instead, getting immersed in a political trip.

The Psychedelic Rangers also believed the Aquarian Age would bring about the brotherhood of man. The teachings of the prophet Jesus Christ were supposed to be actualized in the Age of Aquarius. Humanity would be reborn. A new consciousness of mankind had arrived, or so they believed.

John Starr Cooke, as Van was telling me, felt that the tarot was an important aspect of this change.

Like John was really into the tarot, man. The Tarot, he said, isn't a tool for fortune tellers; it's a path that can help your spirit to unite with God. Self unites with self, you dig. It's all about the Royal Maze, man, and the great paradox is that to get out of it, you gotta get into it. We're all on a journey in this world, man, but the Tarot will take us a lot further. And this is all about being.

Then he showed me some of the Tarot trumps, or books that he drew and painted, according to this entity called ONE. Really far out, man, and I was a little mystified by their symbols: Nameless-One, Royal Maze, Thinker, Feeler, Knower, Reverser, Unity, Actor, Changer, Seeker. . . . He calls the Tarot the royal way, the royal way through life. And like it's a path we all follow.

After Van had left, I thought about what he'd said. Humanity was supposed to be reborn. That's great, right? So what went wrong? What *always* goes wrong? People lacked conviction. They were seduced and led astray. The spirit is willing, they say, but the flesh is weak.

24

As Surrealistic as a Pillow

Wow! Now this is a great album! Everybody loves *Surrealistic Pillow*. February first was declared a community holiday in the Haight-Ashbury, because that was the day it was released. Larry Miller turned a lot of people on to groovy music on KMPX when he brought about an underground format with his off-the-cuff comments, never (as far as we know) kowtowing to the demands of an uptight, conservative, rightwing, Republican manager. Working graveyard from twelve to six, eclectic Larry brought the San Francisco sound to FM radio. We liked Tom Donahue, too. He arrived at the station a little after Larry.

Almost all the people I knew had Jefferson Airplane's second album. We loved Jefferson Airplane and all the musicians; not the managers, but the musicians. Unfortunately, I never had much money when I lived on Waller Street, so I didn't buy albums. Besides, I didn't have a stereo or even the most ordinary record player, so there was no point. But I did have a radio, and listened to KMPX, which, at the time, was a revolution in music, and more fun than listening to AM radio and Lesley Gore, who had a nice voice, but the wrong manager.

Everybody in the Haight loved "My Best Friend" for a lot of reasons: the harmony, the orchestration, the lyrics, and especially the good vibes it communicated. We didn't care if it wasn't a national hit, because it was a hit in the Haight, epicenter of the psychedelic counterculture. But we liked the whole album: "She Has Funny Cars," "Somebody to Love," "My Best Friend," "Today," "Comin' Back to Me," "3/5 of a Mile in 10 Seconds," "D.C.B.A.-25," "How Do You Feel," "Embryonic Journey," "White Rabbit," and "Plastic Fantastic Lover." The songs were not all written by the same person; Marty Balin, Grace Slick, Jorma Kaukonen, Darby Slick (of The Great Society), Skip Spence, Paul Kantner and Tom Maslin wrote them.

Of course the title was a godsend. It was like a poem by Guillaume Apollinaire or André Breton. Like the sumptuous texts of the surrealists, *Surrealistic Pillow* seemed to navigate the realm of the subconscious and feature the *non sequiturs* one expected from oneiric experience.

Grace Slick joined the band from The Great Society

when Signe Anderson left the group to take care of her family. Signe sang on the Airplane's first album, *Jefferson Airplane Takes Off.* We liked her voice a lot. Grace's voice was something very special, too. In any case, "Somebody to Love" was the group's first hit record. Grace brought another hit to the group with "White Rabbit," a song she had also written. The imagery of Lewis Carroll's *Alice's Adventures in Wonderland* thrilled the psychedelic counterculture that was into hallucinogenic mushrooms and altered states of consciousness. So many people in the Haight-Ashbury were *so far out there* that they immediately identified with the drug-oriented motifs. The White Rabbit in the book and the song is perhaps a symbol of our search to explore the subterranean depths of reality to find out what is really going on.

Surrealistic Pillow was released during an accelerating stream of music that blended folk and rock guitars with up-beat rock rhythms. The popularity was developed by groups such as the Beatles, Rolling Stones, Byrds, the Mamas and the Papas, Donovan and many others. By the time the album was released, the media had made sure the world knew what the hippies were doing in the Haight-Ashbury, but *Surrealistic Pillow* helped to show the quality of the music that was being created in San Francisco. Big Brother and the

Holding Company, the Grateful Dead, Moby Grape, Quicksilver Messenger Service, Steve Miller and other bands profited indirectly from the Airplane's success. The epic album was released when the Haight-Ashbury was peaking. It was an eidolon of the counterculture's hopes and aspirations, a metaphor of things that could be, if everyone got together. People were enjoying the ride in 1967, but many suspected that it wouldn't last forever.

We could see that the media had a thing for the Airplane, too. With its white, middle-class college look, Jefferson Airplane was the darling of the media establishment. *Look* magazine published an article on the band entitled "Jefferson Airplane Loves You," ageless Dick Clark was hot to get Gracie and the Airplane on American Bandstand, and Tom and Dick Smothers had to have them on the show as soon as possible. No other San Francisco band had made it so big, and the band's future success was assured by the Monterey Pop Festival.

On the album Grace sang and played recorder, organ and piano; Paul Kantner played guitar and sang; Jorma Kaukonen played lead and rhythm guitar and sang; Jack Casady played bass guitar and sometimes rhythm guitar; Spencer Dryden was on drums and percussion instruments; and Marty Balin sang and played the guitar. Jerry Garcia was listed on the liner notes as *musical and spiritual advisor*, which is rather vague. During recording sessions in November of 1966, Jerry cruised down to smog-shrouded LA. Studio logs list him on several songs including "Today," "Plastic Fantastic Lover," "My Best Friend" and "Coming Back to Me." He may have helped out on other songs, too. Jorma Kaukonen was there, so he knew what went down. Rick Jarred was big time in LA, but he didn't know twat about the Airplane and what they were trying to do in music. Jerry Garcia and the Airplane were good friends in the Haight, when the Haight-Ashbury was *really* a community. 710 Ashbury was the-good-vibes-house on the street. Members of the Airplane would go there to smoke some good weed, have a few laughs and jam together. As Jorma said, Jerry was the producer of the album in the real sense of the word. Why? Because "he was one of us," and he knew what the band was going for. Jerry had a lot of experience and *savoir faire;* he could play rock, folk, jug band, bluegrass, you name it, and he could do it right! He could talk about dynamics, arrangements and guitar tracks. Without Jerry in the RCA studios, *Surrealistic Pillow* would have been a lot different, and that's the truth. Jerry played lead or acoustic guitar, depending on the song, but it's not over. The mind blower is that he arranged or rearranged "Somebody to Love." Maybe the Airplane had to sneak him into the studio because of company regulations. Moreover, the Dead and the Airplane had signed with different labels. Jerry was with Warner Bros. Records, but the Airplane was with RCA. I suspect the members of the band mistrusted RCA, feeling that they wanted to control the entire artistic process, so they wanted a professional musician and a friendly face they could count on in the studio. That would be Jerry, who did everything he could to help the Airplane make good music. And let's not forget that Jerry gave the band the title to the album. He heard a take and said, "That's as surrealistic as a pillow." And we all know that titles sell records.

That's basically how *Surrealistic Pillow* became an epic album of the counterculture.

25

Four Gurus on a Boat

Some Diggers turned me on to a unique event scheduled to take place in Sausalito involving Timothy Leary, Allen Ginsberg, Gary Snyder and Alan Watts. Places were very, very limited, but I managed to finagle my way in.

As it turned out, the conference, summit, discussion or whatever it was supposed to be, took place on February 5, 1967, on a somewhat rickety nineteenth century houseboat, the S.S. *Vallejo*.

There was a lot of bustling about when I arrived, with media people, including a group from the *Oracle* setting up sound equipment to tape the event.

I knew who the speakers were, but didn't know any of them on a personal basis. I'd seen Leary and Ginsberg at the Be-In and had seen Allen reading some of his poetry in North Beach, but that was all.

I'd read some of Alan Watts's books like *The Joyous Cosmology* (1962) and *The Book on the Taboo against Knowing Who You Are* (1966), and watched his program on KQED. It was fairly common knowledge in the Haight-Ashbury that he'd taken LSD and that he smoked grass, but it was also rumored that he liked to drink. His books on Buddhism were popular in the counterculture because his point of view, language and comparisons were so different from traditional Zen Buddhism.

Timothy Leary, the apostle of LSD, didn't need any introduction at the Houseboat Summit. I'd read *The Psychedelic Experience* (1964) that Tim coauthored with Richard Alpert and Ralph Metzner and *Psychedelic Prayers after the Tao Te Ching* published by the League for Spiritual Discovery (1966).

Allen Ginsberg was one of my favorite contemporary American poets and I'd read *Howl and Other Poems*. A lot of us were motivated to read *Howl* because of the much publicized pornography trial. Allen said he wrote his best poetry when he was stoned, like Charles Baudelaire and Samuel Taylor Coleridge.

Of course I'd seen Gary Snyder with Allen Ginsberg at the Human Be-in and I knew he was into Buddhism, but I wasn't that familiar with his poetry at the time.

It seemed to me that Watts, as host, set the tone of the discussion as he introduced the speakers. Allen Cohen was introduced as representing *The San Francisco Oracle*, "far-outer than any far-out." He presented Allen Ginsberg as a poet and *rabbinic sadhu*, Gary Snyder as a poet and Zen monk, but when he introduced Timothy Leary, he broke out in laughter. I found it annoying and it obviously embarrassed Tim. The people at the *Oracle* must have complained about it because Leary was idealized by the underground paper.

Those of us in the audience didn't see why it was necessary to do so, but Watts underscored the fact that the panelists were not political radicals from the East Bay. Everybody knew he was referring to Berkeley.

So what was going to be discussed? Apparently the big issue was whether to "drop out," alluding to Leary's slogan, or simply "take over." Tim was quick to respond to that by saying anything in between should also be discussed, and Watts concurred.

In this sort of a panel discussion it's interesting to see who dominates. Gary Snyder and Timothy Leary spoke more than Watts or Ginsberg, and Gary Snyder seemed to have an axe to grind with the former Harvard Professor. I don't know if Allen Ginsberg felt intimidated or what, but he tended to be passive during the discussions. Watts, as moderator, may have felt that it would have been inappropriate for him to dominate the discussions, though he did make numerous comments throughout the Summit. I felt that the speakers often got sidetracked by trying to develop certain details, and that they were showboating to emphasize their scholarship.

Gary Snyder was the youngest of the group at thirty-seven, so the gurus of the summit weren't baby boomers by any stretch of the imagination. Alan Watts, of British origin, had not completely lost his British accent or diction, although he'd been living in the United States for a number of years. His animosity for the establishment was obvious and may have been inflamed by his conflicts with American culture and mores.

During the discussions a comparison was made between political pacifists and religiously oriented hippies. Pacifists were depicted as wanting to move crowds with feelings of anger or moral outrage. Timothy Leary said he wanted no part whatsoever of mass movements, in other words mass political movements, justifying his position by saying that politics was meant for power-trippers. Politicos should drop out and turn on, said Tim. He did, however, advocate Be-Ins, which would necessarily be mass social and cultural movements.

According to the houseboat gurus, political radicals were antithetical to the psychedelic movement, which, in their minds, was on a religious quest. Nothing was more violent than peace movements and agitated pacifists, said Watts. Tim, for his part, was pissed off at the "men with menopausal minds," an image that stuck in the minds of the audience like shit to a shovel.

I doubt that I was the only person there who felt the speakers were often ambiguous and that sometimes their arguments were irrelevant and tainted with sophistry. Did they *really* believe that flowers, beads, chanting and bellbottoms could change the world?

"Turn on, tune in, drop out," Tim's pet slogan was reiterated throughout the discussion. But who really knew what he meant? The panelists spoke about change, but how could you change anything if you didn't know what you wanted to put in its place?

Alan Watts boldly claimed that the underground had no leadership. Was the Human Be-In in Golden Gate Park a good example of that premise? Watts pursued this idea by saying nobody was in charge as a ruler. This assertion bothered me, because the people on the platform addressing the audience had to be in charge of the happening. When people are on a stage they are going to be in charge of communication. The people on the stage and/or platform were acting as performers. The audience was essentially passive, as far as that was concerned. The same thing could be said of the Haight-Ashbury, where a group of elite hippies was in charge of communication, entertainment and decision-making, and that included the Diggers, the H.I.P. merchants, the dance concert promoters and other groups.

Allan Watts had a positive view of Chinese culture. He argued that the Chinese view of the world, if such a thing really exists, is organic, by which he meant there was no God as boss. Within a philosophical framework that might be true, but certainly not in a political framework. Chairman Mao Zedong, the Chinese Communist leader, had murdered millions of his countrymen. Similarly, Watts said there was no *bossism* in the counterculture. That, too, is a subject open to debate, but there was no debate during the Houseboat Summit, just a series of controversial assertions.

To my way of thinking the four speakers were definitely leaders of the psychedelic counterculture. Sure, they could claim they never proclaimed themselves leaders, but they didn't have to. According to the mass media, the underground media and the hippies, they were *de facto* leaders in the sense that they created the orientation for the psychedelic movement, and evoked the guiding principles and moral standards.

The doctrine about dropping out of society, espoused by Doctor Leary, was hotly debated. Allen Ginsberg pointed out that Tim hadn't dropped out at all. In fact, he hadn't dropped out of Harvard because he'd been thrown out. It occurred to me that pretty much everyone, including the four gurus, was tied to the economic system. They all had their bills to pay and were all working for money, in one way or another, and so were tied to the capitalist system. It could also be argued that they were making money on the hippie counterculture, even if their intentions were basically noble.

Tim loved to criticize the mass media and used the expression *robot establishment*. But at the same time he didn't object to using the mass media to advance his personal agenda and add to his notoriety. That made me think about his work at Millbrook. I'd never been there, but from what I'd heard and read, it seemed to me that it too could be described as a "fake, prop, television set" social group, because some people were behaving the way they were expected to behave, and in that sense were playing a game that might be called the Millbrook game. But again, I'd never been there and had seen no point in going, even if I could have.

Members of the counterculture, of which I was a member, or at least felt I was, needed to think about surviving like everyone else. So was *dropping out* really possible? In a capitalistic society, or any type of modern, industrial society, you had to buy food, pay your bills, pay for your books and tuition if you were a student, pay for your transportation, your grass, and so on. Where was the rent money going to come from once you had dropped out? And if education was just an "addictive process" that Leary advised people to drop out of, who was going to do the educating? What is the best way to educate people so that society has competent professionals working for the betterment of all concerned? Who is going to train the doctors, lawyers, teachers, engineers, skilled technicians, programmers or architects? No guru could give a person a crash course on such things, neither could Tim's Death of the Mind show at Winterland. Could subculture institutions fill the void, as Gary Snyder believed? If they could, they would probably end up mimicking the institutions that Snyder rejected.

When Tim advocated putting all America's technology underground, I thought at first it was a pun, but no, he was dead serious. Images of Fritz Lang's *Metropolis* and the deprived epsilons of Huxley's *Brave New World* shot through my mind. *Metropolis*, I remembered, depicts a world where an oligarchy rules over the proletarians that slave underground in the great factories to keep the machines going.

The question of dropping out or taking over was brought into the discussion again. I noticed that Leary was mitigating his earlier assertions by saying everyone would decide how and when they would do it. Watts said those who dropped out would be "the sages in the mountains" who would constitute an "elite minority." Would this *elite minority* be taking care of the decision making? None of the panelists believed that everyone could drop out. Maybe, suggested Watts, there would be a large unemployed class who would simply be paid to buy the products of the machines. Would they make up the technologically unemployable in this new utopia? How would it be financed? What would be the consequences of such a system? Would the hierarchy they were suggesting be immutable? No one offered an answer, probably because they hadn't thought it out.

As a result of turning on and dropping out, the human race would become happier and healthier than the "ants" and the "bees" described by Tim, or so it was assumed. Those who had abandoned the anthill and the beehive would represent the New Age tribal culture. They would be the enlightened ones, at least in theory. It might take about three generations or so, but the minds of the children in this New Age would be completely reconditioned. The family would change, too, with parents having fewer children and consuming less.

All industry would be centralized around the Chicago area, and the rest of the United States would become "buffalo pasture." When I heard that I was sure the four sages were talking through their hats, just saying whatever bubbled out of their subconscious minds. In that sense the buffalo chips were getting stronger and stronger smelling as they filled up the house boat. Naturally, driving cars would be outlawed in the pastoral utopia; besides, people wouldn't want to drive cars anyway. I guess the sages would take America back to the good old days when pioneers traveled in Conestoga wagons to get where they wanted to go.

But as I studied the speakers' expressions and listened to the tone of their voices, it was fairly obvious they were putting us on. I also assumed that they were peaking on whatever it was that they had ingested before the Summit, because I'd often heard the same sort of supercilious banter coming from less sophisticated individuals. The words they were speaking couldn't have been coming from the brain, but merely from the larynx or their vast reservoirs of dissatisfaction with the American Dream, not that I was defending that archaic myth that was conceived to sell the masses on capitalism. I think the people in the audience understood, too, because I could see them smirking in disapproval.

And then Snyder pulled out the ace up his sleeve by mentioning Kroeber's *Handbook of the California*

Indians. That sent the gurus reeling. They struggled to find their rhetorical equilibrium as the discussion shifted gears. *Get back to nature* they intoned with satisfaction. Like the freaks of the Haight-Ashbury, the panelists knew that the Native Americans had been right all along. Who else could achieve peace and harmony with the environment? Certainly not the Cartwrights in *Bonanza* or Matt Dillon in *Gunsmoke*.

Americans would live in great tribes. Did they mean like the Cherokee, Apache, Hopi, Cheyenne, Comanche and Mohican tribes? The Native Americans, massacred by European immigrants, did represent a model for environmental harmony, but I couldn't picture most Americans living in communes or on reservations either. That was a hippie idea.

Perhaps meditation centers needed to be set up around the country, and more Human Be-Ins needed to be organized to enlighten the half-witted masses. I didn't think learning to meditate would be bad, on the contrary, but that seemed to be antithetical to the type of consumer society the establishment was perpetuating and sought to perpetuate.

Would Americans want to abandon the nuclear family and accept group marriages? "Capitalism is doomed and civilization goes out," said someone. The panelists burst out in spontaneous guffaws. Personally,

I knew that the commune represented an idealized mythos in the counterculture, a New Jerusalem, so to speak, but hopefully with greater freedom. And certainly the hippie communards tried to represent expanded consciousness: *do your own thing in your own time*. So, if I understood the speakers correctly, the communards were enlightened, while the "ants" and the "bees" were doomed to a life of drudgery. I'd been to a few communes, and what I'd seen, for the most part, was far from being idyllic. Simply going to a commune, in the city or in the country, would not necessarily change a person's mindset or psychology. Wherever they go, people usually take all their neuroses and game playing with them. Selfishness, sexism, jealousy and subjugation were not alien to Shangri-La. Operating a successful commune requires organization, goodwill and pragmatism. Many of the young people I saw dreamed of living in communes so they could have a lot of sex and just goof off the rest of the time. Communes with too many people with that mentality failed. Many communes, too, attracted people with lots of personal and social problems: criminals, drug addicts or alcoholics looking for an easy way out.

Documenting their specific codes, sacraments and types of worship, was seen as an important means of legal protection by the panelists who firmly advocated the use of religion as a good way of structuring the communes. Timothy Leary, who had established his own religion based on LSD, urged everyone to do the same. Underground papers sympathetic to the values of the psychedelic counterculture could print information on how to set up one's own religion.

My general impression of the Houseboat Summit was one of dissatisfaction. There was too much facetious banter and sophistry for what was billed to be a serious conference. The speakers couldn't cut through the gobbledygook and give coherent, straight answers to the issues. Except for Allen Ginsberg, they appeared to be on power trips. Did Doctor Leary *really* believe that ten men could change the entire world in just one year? What kind of men and what kind of government? I could only conceive of dictators being able to do that. I couldn't imagine that coming about in any democracy, and certainly not in the United States where Congress finds it difficult to agree on almost everything.

Some of the things the speakers said appeared terribly naïve to my ears. People were not interested in (material) things but in states of mind, said Gary Snyder. He seemed to be projecting his own value systems and beliefs onto the hippie masses. Oh sure, some people were definitely interested in higher states of consciousness, but from what I could tell, they were few and far between. Many of the freaks I saw taking psychotropic drugs were doing it to feel good or to freak out, not to attain a higher level of consciousness. For many, the drug scene was purely recreational, like drinking beer or wine.

I didn't feel that the Summit (if that's what it was), added to any real understanding of some of the big issues of the time. It was more or less a kind of theatrical performance. That didn't stop me, however, from enjoying the lectures given by Watts on Zen, or the poetry of Allen Ginsberg and Gary Snyder, or some of the writings by Timothy Leary.

The Summit might have been more successful if each speaker had given a prepared talk on a specific topic, with a question and answer period after each speaker. The theme of the conference should have been announced in advance. As it was, the whole thing was a hodgepodge of chaos and incoherency. There wasn't any agenda. I know the counterculture is hung up on organization, but without some form of organization that most people can agree on, it's difficult to achieve anything worthwhile. The Human Be-In was organized by a group of people who decided who would do what and when, even if there was a certain amount of leeway and spontaneity. Without organization it's difficult to print an underground paper, serve free food in the Panhandle, put on a dance concert, give medical care to hippies who need it, plant a garden in a commune and house people living in the street.

26

Satan's on Cole Street

Did Satanism exist in the Haight-Ashbury? This is a difficult subject to discuss, and, admittedly, I'm no expert in this field. There had been some rumors of satanic worship in the neighborhood. I was taken aback by such claims, but when some people invited me to a satanic ceremony in a house on Cole Street, I decided to go and have a closer look. I was naïve at the time, but there were undoubtedly some characters who didn't believe in the peace and love ethos? I tried to keep an open mind, anyway.

When I got to the house there were some people standing outside with candles. I showed them a handout that I'd been given about the group. They looked at it carefully and then at me and said things would begin in a moment, and that I should wait there with them until everything was ready. After a while someone at the top of the stairs of the old Victorian house gave a sign and we climbed the steps. Once inside we descended the stairway leading to the cellar.

It was the first time I'd ever seen a room painted all black. It was a large cellar that must have stretched the entire length of the house. The room seemed to be mostly lit by candles, but there was a red light in the front, near the altar. There were about forty folding chairs in neat rows facing the altar. I took a seat in the last row, trying to be inconspicuous. Some rather mystical flute music introduced the organizers of the event, preceded by the rhythmical beating of a drum.

Six people in different colored robes with arcane symbols on them appeared on the sanctuary and stood around the altar. One man picked up a chalice and solemnly drank its contents before speaking.

Oh Angel of Light, hear my words, for I invoke thee, Sacred Light within myself. Show those present your Truth, that we may know the hidden secrets of this material world. Bring us your Light, that we may illuminate others with the Black Flame of Eternal Truth. Give strength to the Angel and Daemon within each of us. May we enjoy the fruits of our indulgence oh giver of Light for you represent our Earthly existence. Illuminate us with your great wisdom. May we share love with those of our kind and not be tempted to waste it on the unworthy. When wronged, we shall vow vengeance. Angel of Light, you are our guide and model for you represent man, the most destructive of creatures. We shun the hymns of hypocrites and savor our knowledge with great satisfaction. Tonight we praise thee as we praise the prophets of your light, Aleister Crowley, Anton LaVey, John Dee, Michael Aquino and all those who have shared your light. (the audience repeats the speaker's words) Hail Lucifer! Hail Satan! Give us your eternal light!

Now those who wish to take the sacrament may come forward to prove their devotion.

Almost everyone rose and proceeded to go to the altar. I asked a person rising near me what it was. She said it was the Biscuits of Light, and added that they usually contained menstrual blood, sperm and vaginal fluids. When I heard that I figured I'd pass up the occasion, so I remained seated, thinking to myself that I could claim I was taking some medication or something and couldn't eat for a few hours.

When everyone was seated, the service began again. The Satanists gave a kind of sermon on the precepts of their religion.

Sexual freedom for all living human beings is required of us. Lucifer, who brought us eternal light stolen from the house of the gods, wants us to have fun. (tittering in the audience) The bringer of eternal light does not care what our preferences are, if you're heterosexual, bisexual, gay or lesbian, the eternal Light says we should not suppress our sexual orientation, but must enjoy sex to the fullest.

Afterwards members of the sect were encouraged to come forward and relate their latest experiences. It was more or less a potpourri of orgies, sexual encounters, blasphemies of different sorts, perversions, adulteries, propaganda and satanic idolatry, with each member seemingly trying to outdo the others. Some of the claims about the casting of spells, animal sacrifice and invocations of demons became so preposterous that I *really* expected the Three Stooges to step up on the platform and do one of their crazy slapstick routines, with Curly making all his weird noises and faces.

Coming to the end of the service, the leaders asked their followers to spread the Light, insisting on the importance of *not* being influenced by the propaganda of other religions. They also implored everyone to leave a generous contribution to show their devotion to Satan, because he was watching them. I left what I could, which is to say a few pennies and a nickel, figuring that even Satan had his bills to pay.

Walking down the street an image of Prometheus, the mythical character who stole the eternal fire from the gods, came to mind.

The versions of the myth vary, but several accredited

the Titan god with bringing civilization to the human race and even creating humanity from clay. As a result of his theft, Prometheus was punished for eternity by being bound to a rock and having an eagle devour his liver, the seat of his emotions, every single day.

Aleister Crowley, the English Satanist, it so happened, was being honored in an event entitled Invocation of My Demon Brother. Kenneth Anger and other Satanists had rented the Straight Theatre (actually not so "straight") for a show. Van Meter and Scott Bartlett did a light show based on scenes from Anger's film in progress and Crowley's tarot cards. It flopped. The Haight-Ashbury was not into Satanism. The film, lacking in good taste, merely showed Bobby Beausoleil in ridiculous shots. Later, the film was said to be stolen and all eyes turned to Anger's roommate, Bobby Beausoleil, who, nevertheless, denied the allegations. In truth, nobody I knew in the Haight really cared because Anger was thought to be too far out there. The show didn't make any money, and Anger, who was totally pissed off, signed a check for $666.66 to pay for renting the theatre. We all thought that was funny because 666 is the mark of the beast.

That night I had a horrible nightmare. In it I saw a dictatorship ruling over the entire world, with TV screens everywhere and people swearing allegiance to a satanic dictator. They had a cabalistic mark on their foreheads that seemed to glow. There were also revolutionary groups that refused to bow down to the dictator and accept his mark, but they were being exterminated. They lived in hiding, out of fear of being caught by the sinister squadrons of police dressed in black. There were people in handcuffs, too, or something that resembled handcuffs, who were forced to get the mark. Everything was dark and smoky and you could taste the ash and feel the heat from the great fires that lit up the atrocious scene. Everywhere people were wailing and screaming . . . and then, suddenly, I woke up in a sweat, looking around the room anxiously to see if it was real or just a dream. It took me a few minutes to realize it was a dream.

27

Sgt. Pepper's

Everyone was gabbling about or listening to *Sgt. Pepper's Lonely Hearts Club Band.* In the words of one wiped out disk jockey, "This is gotta be the most mostest ever mosted!" We'd never known anything like it. Rambling through the Haight you could hear it blaring from bay windows as if in anticipation of the summer solstice. As I recollect there was still some controversy at the time because of Lennon's remark the year before about the group being more popular than Jesus, but most misunderstood what he meant. Of course the crazies went crazy, as they usually do, burning records (and probably a few books to boot like the Nazis) with right-wingers calling for a ban of the Fab Four. Religious bigotry is always good at inciting hatred and violence.

I'd never seen the Beatles in the States–there were far *too* many screaming girls–but I'd seen them at the Olympia with my girlfriend. I remember that the show was plagued with fights and a few blown fuses. People were even throwing chairs and jumping out of the balcony. In the summer of '66, the band was fed up with concerts because they couldn't play their music, and so they drifted apart.

Haight hippies liked to trip out on the album cover. Not everyone knew who the different people were, but research had begun. For my part I recognized Mae West, Lenny Bruce, Aleister Crowley, W. C. Fields, Edgar Allan Poe, Carl Jung, Fred Astaire, Bobby Zimmerman, Aubrey Beardsley, Aldous Huxley, Dylan Thomas, Tony Curtis, Marilyn Monroe, William Burroughs, Stan Laurel and Oliver Hardy, Karl Marx, H. G. Wells, James Joyce, Marlon Brando, Oscar Wilde, Tyrone Power, Johnny Weissmuller (Tarzan), Stephen Crane, George Bernard Shaw, Lewis Carroll, T. E. Lawrence (Lawrence of Arabia), Sonny Liston, Shirley Temple, Einstein, Bette Davis, Marlene Dietrich, and, of course, the Beatles disguised as Sgt Pepper's Lonely Hearts Club Band.

The Haight flashed conniptions when the vinyl was released because it seemed to represent the psychedelic experience in a neighborhood that echoed *a splendid time for all*. Art had somehow managed to climb up the ladder to the level of psychedelic music. That's right! The Beatles had left pop music in the recording studios and attained a higher level of consciousness. Maybe the barefoot hippies were right after all, that Western civilization would become psychedelicized and start loving everybody. *All you need is love*, right? Didn't Doctor Psilocybin himself say that the Fab Four were nothing less than *avatars of a new world order?* Menopausal minds would all be confined to their rest-home realities.

Sgt. Pepper's was tangible proof that the lads from Liverpool had embraced psychedelics. *We'd love to turn you on.* The entire album was fanfare for LSD, wasn't it? "Lucy in the Sky with Diamonds." Or was it just an innocent drawing by sweet little Julian? The imagery was all about a psychedelic trip, or so it seemed. Tangerine trees and all those rich colors that are the stuff that psychedelic dreams are made of. And what about George's Indian music with the tablas, sitars and all the rest? Really trippy music that hippies listened to when they were looking for *girls with kaleidoscope eyes.* Everyone was getting *high with a little help from their friends.* Even Paul had dropped acid, a drug the Haight-Ashbury knew a thing or two about. Wasn't it all about dope, the *Zeitgeist* of the sixties? Maybe we should ask Mr. Kite, who was flying pretty high himself.

But the counterculture was inspired by more than

just drugs, and was able to appreciate *Sgt. Pepper's* as an *avant-garde* artistic achievement in the fullest sense: musical, visual, mystical and thematic. The album coalesced with the psychedelic inspiration of changes. It was released when the counterculture was peaking on its revolutionary trip that Albert Hofmann set in motion. Most of what it said, in fact, was unconscious more than anything else. Without explicitly saying so, it was against the War in Vietnam that everyone saw as a waste. *Sgt. Pepper's* said it was important to open up and make life better. Everyone could and should do his part. It reminded us, too, that life was short, and that we could *get by with a little help from our friends*, but that we shouldn't wait until we were sixty-four.

As I walked down Ashbury Street I saw a barefoot girl with flowers in her hair and kaleidoscope eyes, and so I said, "Hello! Hello! You must be Lucy in the Sky with all those diamonds in your eyes." She took a daisy out of her cinnamon hair, held my hand and gave me a Hashbury kiss that stimulated my hormones and expanded a lot more than my consciousness. But before I could say *love is all you need*, she was gone.

28

The Dead's First LP

Before *Sgt. Pepper's* was released the Grateful Dead were working on their first LP. *The San Francisco Oracle* advertised the album in issue number seven, "The Houseboat Summit." It was a full-page spread with the names of the members–Bob Weir, Pigpen, Bill Kreutzmann, Jerry "Captain Trips" Garcia and Phil Lesh. All the songs were listed, side one and side two, "The Golden Road," "Beat It on Down the Line," "Good Mornin' Little School Girl," "Cold Rain and Snow," "Sittin' on Top of the World," "Cream Puff War," "Morning Dew," "New, New Minglewood Blues," "Viola Lee Blues." The album was produced by Dave Hassinger, the engineer was Dick Bogert, and the cover design was by Mouse Studios.

I'd seen a couple of the group's concerts and knew they were going places, but figured they'd be going through a few changes along the way.

I wanted to learn a little more about the LP, so I put

my stash of Panama Red in my pocket after rolling a few joints, bought a gallon of red wine and headed for 710 Ashbury Street and the Grateful Dead. It was a sunny afternoon in the City and the vibes were mellow. When I arrived at their pad, there seemed to be this party going on, right on the front steps of their Victorian home.

I didn't want to be pretentious, so I just said it was a groovy day to be alive, handed Pigpen the wine, lit a couple of doobies and passed them around. All the members were there, as far as I could tell, and some of the Airplane, too, Kaukonen, Grace and Kantner.

I congratulated the group on their album and said I'd seen them play a couple of times, just to prime the pump to get the conversation going. Sure enough, I didn't have to say much because they were talkative. They said it was a wild, rush affair in Hollywood, a place I knew fairly well. A number of their remarks about the whole thing were sardonic. Of course San Francisco and Los Angeles have totally different mindsets about a lot of things, and the bands from the Haight are generally mistrustful of LA and the way things are done there. The remarks about RCA studios were disparaging, but I reassured them by saying that perfidious reptiles can be found anywhere.

The band members said they were rushed during the

recording and didn't have anything positive to say about Hassinger, the producer, who was organizing things as if he had a time clock up his butt. He'd already produced the Rolling Stones, so, I don't know, maybe the Dead didn't feel like they could object to his way of doing things. There were, however, confrontations from the word go, but Hassinger fit in real well in LA, with his carotene tan, mohair sweaters, razor cut hair and golf ball teeth. One guy took a swig from the wine bottle and said it was like Dick Clark trying to get a hard on, and that the Clydes in LA had ping pong balls for testicles and a plastic dildo for a prick. That got a good laugh out of all of us.

Apparently what Hassinger didn't understand was that the Dead's music was *not* psychedelic. Although they'd probably eaten more acid than the rest of Hashbury, one couldn't consider their music to be psychedelic. Jimi Hendrix was psychedelic, Big Brother and Cream were psychedelic, but the Dead, for the most part, didn't play that kind of music.

The Grateful Dead likes to play long songs, sometimes more than thirty minutes, so when Warner edited a few of the tracks to make them shorter, the band naturally got pissed off. But what can you do? Unfortunately, the Dead's music didn't really sound like the Grateful Dead because of the way it was engineered and recorded.

The trippy album cover was a collage designed by Alton Kelley, with esoteric lettering done by Stanley Mouse Miller. Both Kelley and Mouse excelled in poster art and had done a lot of work for the dance concerts in the Haight. The first text, taken from the *Egyptian Book of the Dead*, read "In the land of the dark the ship of the sun is driven by the Grateful Dead." Jerry and the band decided to change the wording because it was way too grandiloquent for them.

I rolled a few more doobies, took a couple of hits on one, and passed them around to eager fingers. Someone asked me what the bad shit was. "Panama Red," I replied. He told me they were used to smoking Acapulco Gold, but liked the taste and the trip of the weed. "You guys must know that, according to rumors, John smoked the devil's weed." And then I suggested they turn on LBJ and HHH. Looking at amazing Grace, I said she might want to dose them with something stronger. Did I detect a Prankster's gleam in her eyes and a mischievous smile on her lips? *All of those suckers need to be dosed, so they can get their fuckin' minds straight*, I thought I heard her say. "Right on! Right on!" said others.

The tempo of the songs, said a couple of members, was faster than usual, and didn't reflect what they usually did in concert, or in the Panhandle, when they performed for free. So I asked why the tempo was so fast. Some said it was because the band was taking Mountain Girl's diet pills, which were made with amphetamine. Another reason, someone said, is that if the band finished the album early, they could keep the money that wasn't spent. Warner, they said, wasn't going to put its hand in its pocket again, at least not until they came out with another LP. And the band had a lot of mouths to feed, equipment and grass to buy, and rent to pay.

At that point MG said the producer was this plastic dude who was falling all over himself to be cool, but the band was hassling him and saying that all his suggestions wouldn't sound right. She also said the album was the one she liked the best because that was when she and Captain Trips began groovin' together at seven-ten.

In early April, KMPX, an FM radio station, completely changed the traditional format of broadcasting by playing longer songs without the annoying disk jockey jibber-jabber. Tom Donahue, who was working at the station in the evening, helped to promote the album by playing both sides on his show. Although that helped the Dead to become a household word in the Bay Area, the record wasn't selling too well anywhere else. But that was probably due to a lack of imagination on the part of the record moguls.

At that point Captain Trips and the other guys got out their guitars and started jamming an impromptu version of "The Golden Road," with Pigpen on harmonica and Grace doing vocals. And that's something I'll never forget.

29

South to Monterey

When word got out about the Pop Festival scheduled for the sixteenth to the eighteenth of June, everybody wanted to go. Tickets were priced from $3.00 to $6.50, which was proof to me that the Festival was about making money. That didn't really surprise me because the organizers were from Southern California and the LA area, which is distinctly different from Northern California. As usual, I didn't have any money for tickets, but I wanted to go anyway, figuring that I might be able to sneak in or that maybe some of the shows would be for free (ha! ha!), so I took my sleeping bag and my small tent and hitched a ride south on Friday.

Luckily, I got there before evening and had to scramble to find a little space on the football field where I pitched my tent. Monterey was already crawling with people to take in what promised to be a mammoth event. Hippie vans and busses came from Vancouver, Seattle, Oregon, Nevada and well beyond.

A number of young people, who had traveled across the country to go to the Haight-Ashbury for the Summer of Love stopped off in Monterey to check it out. Most of the people I talked to were there to see the San Francisco bands–Jefferson Airplane, Grateful Dead, Big Brother and the Holding Company, Steve Miller, Quicksilver Messenger Service, Moby Grape and Country Joe and the Fish from Berkeley–but they really wanted to catch Jimi Hendrix, the Who and some of the other established groups, too. It was obvious that the Festival could never have gotten off the ground without the San Francisco bands.

I'd been to Monterey a couple of times, but I didn't have any contacts there. Like everywhere in California, the Indians were living there a long time before the Spaniards arrived. The indigenous Ohlone tribes prospered by hunting, fishing and gathering different kinds of plants. In the twentieth century Monterey had gained a reputation as a good place for painters and writers. Robert Lewis Stevenson, John Steinbeck, Robert Heinlein and Henry Miller once lived there.

The weather never really gets scorching hot in Monterey because of the ocean, and the summer nights are often cool and damp. In fact, it's usually hotter in September than in July or August. If you dig hiking, there are some far out trails to discover, with breathtaking views of the Pacific Ocean; the Scenic Road Walkway is one of my favorites.

A carnival-like atmosphere dominated the fairgrounds in the early evening. People were smiling, laughing, singing and having fun. You could smell the dope and a lot of people were soaking wet from the *purple rain.* Good vibes overall. Even the Angels refused to storm the place, but the local sheriff kept his eyes peeled for the bikers. The slickos were slithering in the shadows, doing what wheeler-dealer$ do best.

Band members were diggin' the vibes and rappin' with the other bands they'd never met before.

"Say man, ya know what this place needs?" said one musician, taking a hit off his joint and passing it to the other musician.

"What man?"

"A jam!"

"Hey, that sounds cool, and there's a perfect place for that."

"The floral pavilion," they said together.

Out on the damp football field I was in the end zone, trying to do the impossible, namely sleep. Some guys were running around with flashlights, giggling like Sunday school bandits.

I got out of my tent and asked what was going on.

"Just go to the floral pavilion, there's gonna be a free

gig there," they said.

"Oh, yeah? Right now?" I asked, but they were already gone. So I smoked a roach, put on a jacket and followed the crowd.

Inside the pavilion there was a lot of commotion. People with flashlights were moving stuff around. I found myself a good place to wait, when all of a sudden the amplifiers began blasting electronic sounds and the blinding lights came on. There on stage they were: Jimi Hendrix, David Crosby, Jorma Kaukonen, Captain Trips, Jack Casady, Pigpen. . . . They even prepared a light show, pulsating swirls and bubbles in a wide spectrum of colors. The audience was stunned. I was diggin' the sounds when somebody said they were jamming over on the football field, too. When I got there I could hear Pete Townshend, Eric Burdon and the Byrds. They were performing from a flatbed and everyone was groovin' to the music.

The feedback I got from people that had paid to see the shows was that Janis was out of sight, and that she set Monterey on fire with "Ball 'n' Chain." Everybody loved Otis Redding, too, saying they'd never seen so much charisma and energy during a live performance. Ravi Shankar received the longest ovation of any of the performers. He asked people not to smoke dope during his set, but many were dosed with purple magic. On the last day the Who and the Jimi Hendrix Experience stole the show, but not in the same way. Towhshend broke his guitar (why not, he's got plenty of those), but he couldn't match Jimi's backward roll or playing his Stratocaster with his teeth. To end his set Jimi torched his guitar on stage.

When people said they were packed in like sardines in front of the stage and couldn't dance, I was glad I hadn't bought any tickets. It's a drag to have to sit down on uncomfortable folding chairs and listen to rock music when you'd like to be on your feet dancing.

The Grateful Dead, who were stuck between the Who and Jimi Hendrix, were pissed off at the close of the Festival. They got even by "borrowing" the outrageously expensive equipment that Fender had donated. They even had time to pick and choose what they needed for a free concert. They were smart enough to cover themselves by leaving a note to say the owners would get it all back in a short time.

Of course the Dead were old hands at putting on free concerts in the Haight. The more spontaneous they were the better, that way the heat couldn't shut them down. The Diggers supplied Haight's *haute cuisine:* Wonder Bread, American Cheese (or something that looked like it) and lettuce soup. *Bon appétit!* The gig was set up in the Panhandle, and of course *nobody* was in charge. The police were baffled because they could find neither the generator nor the persons in charge, so the music went on all afternoon, with Jimi Hendrix and Eric Burdon joining in the festivities. And to top it off, they did the same thing out in Golden Gate Park, with their buddies the Hell's Angels guarding the amps.

When the free concerts were over, the equipment was dropped off at the Ferry Building, but nobody was dumb enough to hang around for the owners to show up. To make a long story short, Robin Hood and his Grateful Dead got away with it scot-free. Moral of the story: do unto others as they do unto you!

30

Crash Landing

At the Monterey Pop Festival there were people from places like Pocatello, Idaho and Jetmore, Kansas. It was obvious they wouldn't be going back to where they lived after Monterey, and that they'd be going north to San Francisco for the Summer of Love. As I looked around at the teeming crowd in Monterey, I realized that the Haight-Ashbury was going to be submerged by tens of thousands of young people looking for a piece of paradise.

Back in early April those who had a stake in the neighborhood were trying to figure out what to do. The Council for a Summer of Love was in part a reaction to the obstinacy of the Mayor to seek some sort of a compromise with the counterculture. In March Mayor Shelley tried to get the city's Board of Supervisors to publicly declare the hippies unwelcome. He wanted draconian health inspections established in the neighborhood on a regular basis because he felt no affinity with the hippies. Along those same lines the city health director announced there would be multiple health inspections. His name was Ellis D. Sox (LSD Sox!), but his name was as far as his psychedelia went. The response to City Hall was quick as the Diggers led a walk-in on Haight Street to tie up traffic, with the crowd of protestors shouting "Streets are for people." That was the sort of thing that drove Shelley and Police Chief Cahill up the wall. Hippies were even threatened with the National Guard if the problem continued, and it was anything but an idle threat. Fluid traffic was more important to city officials than dealing with the perspective of thousands of young people arriving in the city with no place to stay and nothing to eat. As I thought about it, I could not remember anyone in the Haight-Ashbury ever saying anything good about the Police Chief or the Mayor.

It was weird seeing the Gray Line busses slowly cruising down Haight Street as part of their Hippie Hop sightseeing tour, "the only foreign tour within the continental limits of the United States." The bus drivers read the printed text while driving, which seemed dangerous to us, improvised parts of it, misread other parts, and joyfully handed out printed sheets with what the company considered the latest jargon of the psychedelic counterculture. *How utterly exotic!*

Paradoxically, thc Council for a Summer of Love was officially announced that same day during a press conference down the street from where I lived on Waller Street. There was no way of getting in because the journalists, cameramen and photographers took up all the room. This announcement made the Summer of Love official, in a way. People who'd been, for the most part, living in the neighborhood for at least a few years took part; they included the Family Dog, some Diggers, the Straight Theatre, *The San Francisco Oracle,* Kiva, and a few others.

The Council's discourse was well-seasoned with the metaphors of the love generation to tantalize the press.

The Haight-Ashbury community has created the Council for a Summer of Love in San Francisco. Within the Haight-Ashbury population there are many imaginative and creative energies whose spirit extends throughout San Francisco and the world. The people here today represent some of the manifestations of the Haight-Ashbury spirit and healthy activity. They have decided to participate in a Council for a Summer of Love.

We call upon the world to help us celebrate the infinite holiness of life. We ask all who come here to come here in love and we ask all who live here to greet all men with love. The Council is calling for creative love happenings for every weekend throughout the summer. We are calling upon the forces of love, not of hate. We affirm life, love, peace and self-discovery. The Summer of Love celebrates these values.

The local press was happy because they had something to chew on, but that was not the case with City Hall, which, after a lengthy discussion, agreed that the hippies were not welcome in San Francisco. Similarly, a series of ordinances were established to discourage hippies from sleeping in the parks. It was illegal to put up a tent in any park after ten o'clock p.m. and no musical instruments could be played in any park from nine o'clock p.m. to seven o'clock a.m. The Haight-Ashbury hippies retaliated with their spontaneous music happenings. I recall one day in particular when it was raining, a mini concert was set up in an apartment on Ashbury near Haight that drew several hundred people. A patrol car cruising by saw what was going on and pulled up to stop the music. The men in blue were then targeted with an assortment of fruits, vegetables and rotten eggs. Infuriated, the police rampaged down Haight Street with their nightsticks, arresting dozens of youths. I remembered that in school that sort of behavior was called bullying, but on Haight Street in 1967 the police called it riot control [*sic*].

On April first, *Science News* published an article that caught our attention. It said that LSD might be damaging the chromosomes of people who were dropping acid. Panic! Acid heads were freaking out. The normal rate of chromosome breaks was exceeded by people who dropped LSD, or so they said. My friends were wondering if their kids would be born with three heads, five dicks or a dozen tits on their back!

One of the big hits on the radio was "San Francisco (Be Sure to Wear Some Flowers in Your Hair)" by Scott McKenzie (his real name was Philip Blondheim), a good friend of John Phillips of the Mamas and the Papas who'd written the song to promote the Monterey Pop Festival. It was a bouncy tune that made a lot of money, but reception in the Haight-Ashbury was mixed. For one thing it was considered LA's version of the Haight, since Phillips was based in Los Angeles; and the pop style was definitely not part of the San Francisco sound familiar to concert goers. It certainly fueled the Summer of Love by inciting people to go to California, but without providing any means of dealing with their arrival.

At the same time I could see that the atmosphere of the neighborhood had definitely changed, and not for the better. Part of the reason might be explained by the fact that it was hard, if not impossible, to score any good grass or acid; but there were a hell of a lot of amphetamines, and that's not the same trip. Speed could make people uptight and nervous. As the Summer of Love approached, the peace and love ethos was disintegrating. And police were hassling people more and more on the street for stupid things. It was obvious that the vibrations were a lot better around the time of the Human Be-In, which was a watershed for the peace and love generation.

I don't really know, but something bad happened to the Haight-Ashbury. Did anybody see it coming? Things were changing too fast for us to keep up with them. I'd bought some acid from a guy called Superspade. I didn't know his real name, but he was a good guy. He was on a good trip, and he didn't deserve what happened to him. He was murdered. "Faster than a speeding mind," he said to me, as he handed me the acid. He went to Sausalito with a lot of money to score some acid. Later, I learned that his real name was William Thomas. Another dealer was murdered, too. His name was John Carter, better known as Shob. His murderer, Eric Dahlstrom, hacked off Carter's arm above the elbow. It seems that the two murders were linked, as Shob and Thomas were collaborating on a drug deal.

Everything was going downhill in the Haight-

Ashbury, and the bust at 710 Ashbury, the Grateful Dead house, was a harbinger of the radical change in attitudes. On 2 October 1967, a Prankster by the name of Hermit finked on Mountain Girl, who generously gave him some weed. Fortunately for Jerry and MG, they'd left shortly after, so when the police broke into the house, they weren't there to be arrested.

The "Death of Hippie" parade took place on 6 October 1967. The date was symbolic since it was one year after the ban on LSD. The ritualized funeral procession began at dawn in Buena Vista Park and proceeded down Haight Street carrying a coffin filled with hippie fetishes and bearing the inscription: Death of Hippie Freebie, Birth of the Free Man. Of course not everyone believed the hippie movement was over. The I/Thou coffee shop, the *Berkeley Barb* and other underground papers laughed at the Diggers' project.

After the procession the police aggressively swept down Haight Street arresting runaways and young men without draft cards. It was a federal crime at the time not to be carrying one's draft card. Haight Street became a daily confrontation with the heat, and nobody wanted that.

That same day police hassled the Matrix on Fillmore Street in the Marina, because someone had complained about noise. Big Brother and the Holding Company was giving a show when the men in blue arrived, threatening to throw everybody in the paddy wagon for a trip downtown. On a positive note, the band's first album was released in August and was selling pretty well nationally. Of course we all loved it in San Francisco and the Bay Area and knew it would become a classic of psychedelic rock with songs like "Bye, Bye Baby," "Easy Rider," "Women is Losers" and "Down on Me."

Most of us realized that the sun was setting on The Summer of Love, but we didn't want to admit it. The War in Vietnam, however, was raging, with the number of body bags increasing every day. The war declared on the Haight-Ashbury was different, but it was a war just the same.

31

Morningstar Revisited

With all the shit that was going down in the Haight, I needed to get out in the country to be close to nature again, so I went back to Sonoma County and Morningstar Ranch. Curiosity brought me back there because I wanted to see what was happening.

Lou Gottlieb had a dream, but there are those in our world who excel in destroying dreams. Lou dreamed of creating an alternative society, but as I looked around the ranch, I had a feeling that everything was just disintegrating. A lot of his dream was about utopia, a place of perfection where people could be free and enjoy life.

Figuring the best way to find out what was going on was to talk to the people living there, I went to those who were the easiest to approach: Cindy, Kathy, Nevada, Near-Vana, Don King, and a few others. Some of them said problems arose as more and more people arrived, and with them, different values and a multitude of conflicts. There were nearly one hundred permanent residents at the ranch, with large numbers of visitors. People started being neglectful, showing a lack of respect for the place, throwing garbage wherever it seemed convenient. And some Negroes took control of one of the houses and wouldn't let anyone else in. Lou didn't want to show any authority, so things got worse. A motorcycle gang called the Gypsy Jokers, that was sometimes at the ranch, decided to evict the Negroes. A big fight broke out and several people were injured. That resulted in the arrest of at least one person.

There were other problems, too. One girl said she'd been assaulted and raped by a spade. Nobody seemed interested in doing what was necessary to stop that kind of shit, and nobody wanted to call the cops because the commune already had a really bad reputation with the local population.

Some of the problems were caused by people visiting the commune. The anything goes attitude made some people believe they were free to do anything they pleased, and a few were bringing guns into the ranch. The unwritten law was that people would clean up after themselves, but a lot of the visitors didn't follow that general rule, and people didn't want to clean up somebody else's muck. The local inhabitants had grown uptight with the nudity and with seeing small children who appeared to be neglected and living in unsanitary conditions.

Lou always defended Morningstar, saying that the commune was an instruction in survival. The style of living was similar to that of the American Indians, in other words the land was open to anyone. Lou liked to believe that God would take care of things, and that the Divine Spirit was in charge while he was away. But that wasn't happening, nor could it ever happen. Morningstar, he said, is a "living experiment in an alternate society for the technologically unemployable." Moreover, he argued that communal living was psychologically healthy for a lot of people living there.

At times, there may have been a sense of God consciousness at the commune, but a feeling of irresponsibility was also manifest. Not having any rules or regulations might work when people were responsible, but that didn't seem to be the case when I went there. I couldn't see how so many people could live together in one place if there wasn't a sense of discipline in a positive sense, meaning looking out for yourself and other people, and just being respectful.

I liked the idea of the commune and voluntary primitivism, but there were too many conflicts for it to be successful. The authorities had already been to Morningstar several times and I was certain the local inhabitants wouldn't give up until the hippies had all been forced out. They didn't like young people whom they considered to be scroungy and lazy, and they would find a way of getting rid of them. The easiest way for them to do that would be to cite the health hazards on the ranch that were fairly conspicuous. That being said, the local authorities could have helped the commune to be a success by giving advice and assistance. But the local inhabitants didn't share the hippie values of free living and didn't lift a finger to help them. Most were ultra-conservatives who thought the communards were immoral drug users. It was the same conflict that opposed City Hall and the hippies of the Haight-Ashbury. It was not hard to imagine the problems that Lou Gottlieb would have to face in the near future. There would be raids by the sheriff and the police, fines, and the local inhabitants would use the legal system to impose injunctions on the owner of the property. In short, Morningstar was doomed.

32

God's on Haight Street

In the early days of the Haight-Ashbury a lot of people who were tripping out on LSD were seeing God, or what they *called* God, anyway. Acid is a heavy gig, a mind-blowing experience that can show you both heaven and hell, because that's what we're made of, so a user must be prepared to see both.

With all this talk about God and LSD I was curious to see what people had to say, so I got in touch with the people I knew to find out what I could with my layman's knowledge on the subject.

One of the first dudes I spoke to in the Haight-Ashbury was a runaway named Brian who left home when his parents decided to put him in a mental institution, because he'd said he'd seen God. He was being protected by some people I knew in the Haight. How I found out about him is too complicated to explain, and isn't very important, so I won't go into it.

Unlike me he came from a well-to-do family. Brian

was sixteen and had never had any problems whatsoever at school or with his parents. He was living with his mother at the time. He was an above average student who had skipped a year in high school and was planning on going to Harvard to major in the social sciences or something like that. He didn't tell me what the circumstances were, but he had taken LSD with some friends, and that experience completely changed his perception of reality. He didn't freak out or anything, on the contrary, he had a really mellow trip. The problem is that it showed him how superficial his parents' existence was. He realized that everything in American society is based on exploitation and that most people spend their entire lives playing destructive mind games. A person who didn't have any financial support was nothing, according to the values of society.

He took about 300 milligrams of LSD and when it started kicking in everything began to look different. The colors and the sounds were a lot more intense, the world was pulsating, and everything around him was connected. Reality was one big vibrating universe, and he understood that he was a part of it. The more he concentrated on that reality, the better he could see the oneness of it all. Subjective value judgments didn't have any particular meaning anymore, because he could see that everything in the universe was interrelated. It was an epiphany for Brian who suddenly realized that everything his school and parents had told him about life was wrong, that it was propaganda to control his mind and his behavior.

His experience was so profound that he had to share it with someone, so he told his mother about it, believing he could trust her. That was a huge mistake because his mother totally freaked out. She realized she couldn't control him anymore. Brian contradicted her lies about society and said her values were superficial. When she saw she didn't have any power over him, she called a psychiatrist, who advised her to send her son to a mental institution for analysis. Brian heard her talking on the phone and saw what she was planning to do, so he took off. Luckily for him he had some friends in San Francisco who were willing to look out for him.

I had an opportunity to speak to Brian and found his perceptions illuminating. He said that when he was high on LSD he could see through the pretense of the adult world that was motivated solely by material gain, but what impressed him the most was the oneness of existence, and that oneness he described as God. Mankind, he felt, had a responsibility to live in harmony with the environment and the other species. That was God's will. But he could see that this was not the case, that people's values were perverted and that it probably would have dramatic consequences for everyone in the future because it created a disequilibrium, and not only on earth, but in the entire universe. This is something that his mother simply could not fathom and said he was delusional.

Brian didn't blame his mother for her obtuseness, but said her consciousness was too limited to see how the universe functioned. I found him to be very rational. He knew that because he was a minor, he couldn't reject his parents completely, but didn't want to be controlled by their narrow-mindedness. "God is love," he said, and this realization changed his life. "From here on out," he said, "I'm going to do my best to live in accordance with God's universal laws, and not be seduced by His shadow."

I've heard others talk about their experiences on acid, and not everyone had a divine or mystical trip by a long shot. But those who did often spoke about the interconnectedness of existence, which is not something people automatically see.

Some people on acid trips have spoken about *ego death*, or dying and being reborn again. A number of acid heads have claimed they'd traveled through the different Bardo planes as described in *The Tibetan Book of the Dead*, with demons in flames trying to grab them, or simply making terrifying noises. Acid heads have claimed it is impossible to soar through the many dimensions, that all you can do is flow with it. Others said one is swallowed up by eternity. They didn't use the words *enlightenment* or *epiphany*, maybe because the trip was just too weird to describe.

Other people who said they'd seen God spoke about an intense white light that was so overwhelming it forced a person to be humble. One felt exposed, they said, as though they could not conceal their thoughts or feelings. A person's entire human existence could be revealed in an instant. The lights described varied to some degree. Sometimes people used the expression *coruscations of light*, but generally speaking, the overwhelming light that appeared before them was white, and far too brilliant to look at because it was blinding.

So what happened after these divine experiences? Most people I spoke to went back to doing what they did before and behaving the way they did before. A few, however, admitted that the confrontation with the divine changed them in their approach to life and in their associations with other people. Some changed their lives completely.

Louis-Bertrand Labeuhe has given us an important document about the Haight-Ashbury in the mid-sixties. We've often thought about what he'd seen in the Haight, what it meant to him on a personal level, what it meant in the context of the sixties, and what it means to us today.

Utopia is not an unusual desire of the human race. Thomas More gave us the word with his sixteenth century classic. But in many ways his book is merely a fantasy; an ideal perhaps, but something the human race would never be able to put into practice anywhere. More's intentions are clear because he coined the word using his knowledge of Greek. The negative prefix means *not* and the root *topos* means *place.* So he's describing "no place," a place that doesn't exist. Since Eutopia and Utopia are pronounced the same way, More is also describing what he believed was a good place, since the prefix "eu" means *good* in Greek. So the good place is also the place that doesn't exist. In other words it's a sort of dream vision, a fantasy of his imagination. Most people wouldn't agree with some things in More's book, because slavery is practiced on the island of Utopia, and there are severe travel restrictions as well because you need a passport to go from one place to the next. And people who refuse to abide by the law are placed in slavery.

Lou Gottlieb called Morningstar ranch "utopia," but people never thought they'd see it in America. Hippies, "people who retired early," went to the Haight-Ashbury because they were in search of utopia, and if they'd arrived a year earlier, they might have found it, but in the summer of 1967 it was too late because there were simply *too* many people living in a small neighborhood. Thomas More was aware of the problems of overcrowding, because in *his* good place, the population of the cities was strictly limited.

If so many young people were in search of something better, it's because they were disillusioned with American society and its values. Many were alienated from a culture that seemed to be based exclusively on material wealth. As more and more of them began using psychedelics, they could see the sham of that kind of existence. That was obvious to almost everyone. The so-called hippies, a word used mainly by the establishment and the straights in a derogatory way, rejected money culture. They didn't want to spend their whole lives doing some meaningless tasks to make someone else or themselves wealthier. Retire when you're sixty-five years old to do what? It's too late, your youth is gone.

Humanity's problem is that it can't conceive of a society that's not based on money. Many of the communes tried to set up a communal existence that wasn't based on capital, but it was difficult. The counterculture in the Haight tried to do it and promote it, especially the Diggers, and they ran into a lot of conflicts, too.

Many groups in the counterculture were aware of the corruptive influence of money. They could see that it coerced human relationships. Nobody could do anything out of friendship, compassion or pleasure, money had to be exchanged. This was particularly obvious at the workplace or when doing work for someone else. It wasn't the quality of the product that was important, but the profits received. Since this was the motivating principle, virtually everything was affected: food, healthcare, education, leisure, transportation, housing, clothing and everything else. The counterculture, for the most part, flatly rejected this idea. Consequently, the establishment sought to undermine and destroy it. That's why J. Edgar Hoover launched a campaign against the underground press for advocating a different or parallel society.

But in fact, money is an artificial creation. When someone is hungry, they need food. When someone is homeless, they need a house. When someone is unqualified, they need education and a teacher. When someone is sick, they need medical care. The monetary system creates a lot of obstacles and it destroys compassion and generosity. So what do you put in the place of money? Nothing. When people are hungry you give them something to eat. When people are sick you give them healthcare. When people want to learn you educate them. When people need a house or an apartment you build one. When people want entertainment you organize a dance concert and put on a show. There's so much work to do that everyone should be able to find something that needs to be done. One important question we need to ask ourselves is *who* profits from the monetary system? That shouldn't be too difficult to answer, so let's move on.

The establishment freaked out about marijuana and drugs in the Haight-Ashbury and elsewhere. But today you can buy weed in many states, and marijuana has been decriminalized in others. A lot of countries have dispensaries, as they call them, where you can buy dope. But in the sixties authorities wanted to put Timothy Leary and other pot smokers away for a long time. So what changed? The establishment realized that there was a lot of money to be made in dope. But the dispensaries and dope shops of today are not at all what people really wanted. It's a capitalist scam. You need a million dollars to open a shop to sell cannabis. Growing six plants at home is not enough. A lot of people feel we've been screwed again, like always. Who the fuck has a million bucks to open a dope shop, anyway? Big money invaded the market and took over again, to the people's detriment.

LSD was the drug that changed things in the Haight, and a lot of people were getting stoned on acid in 1965. That was because of Augustus Owsley Stanley III, the unofficial Mayor of the Haight-Ashbury. In the spring of 1965 he was producing hundreds of thousands of hits. Until he invested in a pill press, when he gave each batch a different color, he distributed his product as a liquid. He became the main supplier in the Haight, which is to say there were others, but Owsley's acid was better because it was purer. Owsley and Tim Scully felt they could change the world by turning people on to acid, and so they sold it cheap and gave a lot away, sometimes to celebrities. In that sense the Haight-Ashbury was an experiment, a prototype of what could be done elsewhere. Dealers had a field day in the Haight, but in the beginning they were like evangelists bringing good news and expanding consciousness.

They were not the first, but they had a huge impact at the time. Unfortunately, those ideas got turned around when money became more important than the public service, and the cutthroat practices began. Feelings of love evaporated as people began getting ripped off and murdered for control of the market. Negative sentiments like selfishness, which had not really existed before in the community, were back again.

The streets belong to the people, right? So what does that mean? That means that in a democracy the people have the right to decide what happens in their neighborhoods. But everybody knows this is not the case. In Greek *demos* means "people", and *kratos* means "rule" or "power," so democracy literally means the people rule. But it seemed obvious that the people didn't decide very much in the Haight. George Orwell, the author of *1984*, described democracy as half a loaf of bread. It's better than no bread at all, which is what you get in Russia, China, Belarus, Myanmar and other totalitarian states.

The hippies in the Haight wanted to live in a different kind of society. They did that to some extent with the way they dressed, the music they listened to, the art they created, long hair, sexual freedom, smoking weed instead of drinking whiskey, not working in boring jobs from nine to five, studying mysticism and the occult arts, and doing things that didn't really interest the mainstream.

People spoke a lot about *freedom* in the Haight and wanting to *do your own thing*. For a lot of people that meant getting stoned when you wanted to, spending the day doing whatever you felt like, going naked in the country, not having to work a straight job, having sex without hang-ups, and so forth. Everybody wants to be free. But in fact, a kind of slavery still exists in our modern, technological society. Most people are forced to work for a salary and do what their boss tells them to do. Money dictates the things they can and cannot do. If you don't show up for work too often, you can get fired. And a lot of people work for slave wages, a fact that often requires them to hold down two or even three jobs just to make ends meet. They don't have any free time whatsoever. If you're a teacher, your choice of subjects is usually determined by the principal or president, the school board, or the state in which you work. If you work for the media–radio, TV, newspaper, Internet, or book publisher–an editor checks what you say and can censure anything he or the owner doesn't like. For students the choices are limited, too. The students at U. C. Berkeley were confronted with that problem when their freedom of speech was arbitrarily denied. Young people in the counterculture preferred to smoke dope instead of getting drunk on alcohol, but they ran the risk of getting busted. Of course freedom also involves a sense of responsibility. Being free doesn't mean a person has the right to hurt someone, do something evil, dishonest or malevolent.

Young people in the Haight used to flash the peace sign with their fingers and say "peace and love." That became a cliché for many, but you can generally tell if someone is sincere or not. In the mid-sixties it was obvious that peace and love were lacking because there were wars going on, both hot and cold, and because people didn't feel empathy, compassion or any need to care about others. Why should they when their parents and the older generation were constantly telling them it was *a dog eat dog world*, and that the best way to become *top banana* was to *never give a sucker an even break*. The world was not at peace in the sixties and it still isn't. Nothing has really changed; not for the better, anyway. Consumer society really screwed up the climate because, unlike the Native Americans, we didn't show any *love* for the environment. Like everything else the human race does, we wanted to dominate and control it, disregarding its own needs.

So if we had really tried to give real meaning to the expression *peace and love*, things could have been a lot different, but the older generation sneered when they heard that. "What are you, some kind of commie?" they'd say. Maybe it's too late for us. Can the human race change? For a lot of us, that's the *real* question. We don't really have an answer, do we? How many people do you know who have radically changed *for the better?*

Chronology

1937	The Marijuana Tax Act is passed, making the possession and sale of the plant illegal in the United States.
1938	Albert Hofmann, a Swiss chemist, synthesizes Lysergic acid diethylamide (LSD).
1943	During WW II, Albert Hofmann accidentally ingests a small amount of the substance and realizes how powerful LSD is.
1951	The Boggs Act establishes mandatory sentences for drug convictions. First offenders can be fined \$20,000 and sent to prison for from two to ten years.
1956	The FBI's COounter INTELigence PROgram (COINTELPRO) is created to investigate suspected subversives.
1957	4 October, the Soviet Union sends the first satellite into orbit: Sputnik.
1958	31 January, the United States sends its first satellite into orbit: Explorer.
1966	9 September, Ronald Reagan announces he will appoint John McCone, former CIA Director, to investigate the campus turmoil at U.C. Berkeley, if elected governor.
1960	9 August, Dr. Timothy Leary eats psilocybin mushrooms in Mexico.
1960	8 November, John F. Kennedy defeats Richard Nixon in the presidential election.
1960	December, birth control pills are sold in the USA.
1960	*Beat Zen, Square Zen and Zen* by Allen Watts; Allen

Ginsberg's *Kaddish*.

1960   Chubby Checker's "The Twist" is released and becomes an instant hit.

1961   In March Richard Alpert takes psilocybin at Harvard.

1961   25 April, the Bay of Pigs invasion in Cuba.

1962   *One Flew over the Cuckoo's Nest* published by author Ken Kesey.

1962   4 August, Marilyn Monroe is found dead.

1962   A television picture is transmitted by Telstar satellite across the Atlantic Ocean.

1962   15 October, the Cuban missile crisis begins after photographs show the construction of Russian missile bases on the island.

1962   Dr. Timothy Leary founds the International Foundation for Internal Freedom to promote psychedelic research.

1963   28 August, Martin Luther King gives his "I have a dream" speech in Washington D. C. at the Lincoln Memorial before a huge, enthusiastic crowd.

1963   Timothy Leary is dismissed from Harvard with Richard Alpert.

1963   More than 700 demonstrations in nearly 200 cities in the Southern USA in protest of segregation.

1963   Timothy Leary moves to Millbrook, New York.

1963   John F. Kennedy is shot dead in Dallas.

1963   *Dr. Strangelove* is released.

1964   Bob Dylan's "The Times They are A-Changin'" is released.

1964   Ken Kesey moves to La Honda.

1964   June, Lenny Bruce's pornography trial begins in New York City.

1964   23 May, Art Kunken founds the *Los Angeles Free Press*

(Freep).

1964   The Civil Rights "Freedom Summer" begins to register Black voters in Mississippi.

1964   10 July, The Beatle's *A Hard Day's Night* is released.

1964   2, 4 August, The Gulf of Tonkin incident in Vietnam.

1964   2 October, the Free Speech Movement is born at the University of California in Berkeley.

1964   10 December, Martin Luther King is awarded the Nobel Peace Prize.

1965   21 February, the assassination of Malcolm X in New York.

1965   6 June, The Rollng Stones' single "I Can't Get No Satisfaction" is released in the USA.

1965   11-16 August, riot in the Watts ghetto in Los Angeles (34 deaths, 8,000 arrests); riots also in Detroit, Chicago, Newark and other cities.

1965   13 August, Max Scherr launches the *Berkeley Barb*.

1965   November 6, Bill Graham organizes the first benefit for the San Francisco Mime Troupe.

1966   3 January, The Psychedelic Shop, run by Ron and Jay Thelin, opens at 1535 Haight Street. It soon becomes a gathering place for the counterculture in the Haight-Ashbury.

1966   March, President Lyndon Johnson signs the Drug Abuse Control Amendment, thus making the mere possession of LSD a felony.

1966   30 June, Richard Helms becomes director of the CIA.

1966   2 September, *P. O. Frisco* is printed in San Francisco. It will become *The San Francisco Oracle*.

1966   20 September, the first issue of *The San Francisco Oracle* is published, edited by John Brownson and George Tsongas.

1966	20 September, A Prophesy of a Declaration of Independence is printed in the first *Oracle,* in protest of the ban on LSD.
1966	6 October, The Love Pageant Rally is held in the Panhandle; the same day that LSD becomes illegal in California.
1966	15 October, Bobby Seale and Huey Newton form the Black Panther Party in Oakland, California.
1966	November, *The Love Book* by Lenore Kandel is seized at the Psychedelic Shop in San Francisco and City Lights Books. A lengthy censorship trial ensues.
1966	8 November, Ronald Reagan, former actor of minor Hollywood films, becomes Governor of California.
1966	17 December, the "Death of Money" street theatre event, with signs that say "NOW."
1967	14 January, the Human Be-In or Gathering of the Tribes is held at the Polo Field in Golden Gate Park.
1967	Friday, 27 January, Leary's The Death of the Mind celebration is held at the Berkeley Community Theatre.
1967	1 February, *Surrealistic Pillow* is released by RCA Victor.
1967	5 February, the Houseboat Summit takes place in Sausalito on the S.S. *Vallejo.*
1967	24 February, The Invisible Circus takes place at Glide Memorial Church in San Francisco.
1967	5 April, the Council for a Summer of Love is announced at a press conference at the old firehouse on Waller Street.
1967	12 May, *Are You Experienced* by the Jimi Hendrix Experience is released. It becomes an instant success.
1967	26 May, *Sgt. Pepper's Lonely Hearts Club Band* is released.
1967	16-18 June, The Monterey Pop Festival opens.

1967	summer, perhaps 90,000 young people go to San Francisco and the Haight-Ashbury.
1967	15 August, Chester Anderson breaks with his partner Claude Hayward of com/co. The split is announced in a text entitled "Hippie Siamese Twins Split." Anderson leaves San Francisco.
1967	25 August, FBI Director J. Edgar Hoover sends a secret document to all FBI agencies detailing how to discredit, manipulate and destroy radical political movements in the USA.
1967	2 October, the Grateful Dead house at 710 Ashbury Street is busted. Only a small amount of marijuana is seized.
1967	6 October, the Death of Hippie procession takes place.
1967	7 November, Joe Alioto is elected Mayor of San Francisco.
1967	December 20, Owsley's laboratory in Orinda is raided and LSD is found.
1968	February, *Oracle* number twelve, entitled "Symposium 2000 A.D. and the Fall," is the paper's last issue. This coincides with the collapse of the Haight-Ashbury.
1968	30 January, the Tet Offensive begins in South Vietnam.
1968	4 April, Martin Luther King is assassinated in Memphis, Tennessee.
1968	5 June, Robert F. Kennedy is assassinated at the Ambassador Hotel in Los Angeles after winning the California primary election.
1968	5 November, Richard M. Nixon wins the presidential election, defeating Hubert Humphrey.

Index